HERS TO KEEP

ANNA STONE

© 2019 Anna Stone

All rights reserved. No part of this publication may be replicated, reproduced, or redistributed in any form without the prior written consent of the publisher.

This is a work of fiction. Names, characters, places, and incidents either are the products of the author's imagination or are used fictitiously. Any resemblance to actual persons, living or dead, businesses, companies, events, or locales is entirely coincidental.

Cover by Kasmit Covers

ISBN: 9780648419235

CHAPTER ONE

"Lindsey," Mr. Grant said. "Can I see you in my office?"

"Sure." Lindsey removed her headset and got up from her desk.

She followed her boss through the call center. It was a honeycomb of identical cubicles, all with the exact same desk, computer, and phone. The walls were painted green, no doubt in an attempt to make everyone forget they were cooped up in a tiny, windowless office for eight hours a day. But the paint had faded to a pale, sickly color, which made it even more depressing.

Lindsey sighed. How had she ended up here? All her life, she'd had such big plans. She was going to be a renowned artist, whose works were displayed in galleries all over the world. She was going to travel to exotic places, and have a string of passionate love affairs before meeting the man of her dreams in some tiny European town. And they'd fall in love and live the rest of their lives in a villa in the countryside.

Then Lindsey had grown up. Well, the world had forced her to grow up.

They reached Mr. Grant's office. Lindsey sat down on the stiff plastic chair in front of his desk.

"I think you know what this is about, Lindsey." Mr. Grant tented his fingers in front of his chest. "Your numbers have been slipping lately."

His voice rang with concern, but just like everything else in this place, it was false. Everyone pretended to give a crap, when really, all they cared about was a paycheck. Lindsey saw through it because she feigned the same enthusiasm around her coworkers and the potential customers she called. She was surprisingly good at this job, at selling lies and convincing unsuspecting retirees to sign up for overpriced insurance. Lindsey didn't like what that said about her.

"Do you want to tell me what's going on?" Mr. Grant asked.

"It's nothing," Lindsey said. "I'm just having an off week."

"It's not just this week, Lindsey. Your performance has been steadily dropping for a while now." He leaned back in his chair. "Do you still want this job?"

"Yes, of course."

Lindsey didn't want it. She needed it. She should have been grateful to have a job at all, let alone one that paid this well. Half her art school classmates were working at Starbucks. Plus, she'd been in a car accident almost a year ago that had left her with a steep medical bill. A few years working at Prime Life Insurance, and she could make a serious dent in her debt.

But the idea of doing this for a few years was soul-crushing.

"You know how it works," her boss said. "We have quotas to meet both individually and as a team. You need to pick things up."

"I know," Lindsey said. "I'll work harder, Mr. Grant."

"Good." He gave her a wide smile that looked more like a grimace. "Why don't you get back to work? I want to see that fresh-faced, energetic employee you were when you started here."

Lindsey left her boss's office and returned to her cubicle. She slid her headset back on and brought up a list of names and phone numbers on her monitor.

As she stared at the screen, all the numbers seemed to blur together. Her dreams seemed more out of reach than ever. She was never going to pay off all this debt, let alone make it to Europe. At age 23, she still hadn't fallen in love. And her sketchbook was at the bottom of a box somewhere, untouched since she finished art school.

Lindsey opened her desk drawer and glanced at the phone inside it. She had a message. The office had a strict 'no cell phones' policy, but she didn't care. Looking behind her to make sure no one was around, Lindsey picked up her phone and read the message. It was from her friend Faith.

Do you have plans tonight?

Just grabbing the last of my stuff from my old apartment, then I'll be right over, Lindsey sent back.

Lindsey's apartment building had been shut down for the foreseeable future because of a dangerous black mold infestation. For now, she was sleeping on Faith's couch. With the housing market in the city as competitive as it was,

Lindsey was struggling to find a place within her budget. She wasn't exactly broke, but money was tight.

Faith's reply came through. *Great! We're going to celebrate the fact that we're roommates again.*

Lindsey grinned. She and Faith had lived together during art school. They'd had plenty of fun together. Not to mention that they'd gotten up to plenty of trouble.

Lindsey looked up from her phone and glanced toward Mr. Grant's office. He was standing by the window, staring straight at her.

Crap. Lindsey stashed her phone in her drawer. She'd better get back to work. She dialed the next phone number on her list.

"This is Lindsey from Prime Life Insurance. How are you today?"

Lindsey fished the spare key to Faith's apartment out of her handbag and unlocked the front door. She dragged her suitcase inside. "Faith? I'm here."

There was no answer, but Lindsey could hear the shower running. She walked into the living room, set her suitcase down, and eyed the old, gray couch that was now her bed. Lindsey had crashed on it several times before. At the very least, it wasn't too uncomfortable. And Faith sometimes stayed overnight with the family she worked for as a nanny, so she'd given Lindsey permission to sleep in her bed when she wasn't coming home for the night.

Lindsey opened her suitcase and rummaged through her clothes. She wanted to change out of her stifling work outfit, but she had no idea what Faith's plans for the two of them involved. Lindsey hoped it was nothing too crazy. It had been a long week, and she was feeling drained.

Faith entered the living room, dressed in sweatpants and a tee, her dark curly hair tied back in a messy bun. She flopped down onto the couch. "All moved in?"

"Yep." Lindsey sat down next to her. "Thanks again for letting me stay with you. I promise I'll be out of your hair soon."

"Take your time," Faith said. "It'll be fun to be roommates again. It'll be just like old times."

"I'll try not to cramp your style when you bring guys home. Or girls."

"I've given up on guys. Girls are much more fun."

"It must be nice to have that choice," Lindsey said. Faith's sexuality, according to her, was that she 'liked people' and that was that. She never bothered to put a label on it. Lindsey envied that about Faith. She always seemed so self-assured.

Lindsey looked Faith up and down. "What's with the sweatpants? I thought we had plans tonight?"

"We do," Faith replied. "We're staying in and doing what we used to do on Friday nights when we lived together."

"You're not serious, are you?"

Faith nodded. "There's some fruit and a bottle of vodka on the kitchen counter. I bought the cheapest bottle I could find. We're making punch and staying up all night."

Lindsey didn't know whether to smile or groan. It had been a long time since they'd gotten drunk together, and for a good reason. It usually ended in disaster. But wasn't

Lindsey just thinking about how boring her life was? Maybe a little excitement was just what she needed.

"Okay," Lindsey said. "Let's do it. But we're ordering dinner first. We don't want a repeat of the first time we did this." That night, they'd both learned the hard way why drinking on an empty stomach was not a good idea.

"Sure," Faith said. "There's this amazing Thai place a few blocks away. And they deliver. Dinner first, then punch. I'll order food, while you get started in the kitchen."

"Deal."

Lindsey got up and went into the kitchen, tying up her long auburn hair on the way. She began to gather the ingredients for their signature alcoholic punch. She and Faith had come up with the recipe in their freshman year. The two of them had been this wild, inseparable pair in college, and their punch recipe had been responsible for more than one crazy night. Since then, they'd outgrown partying, but Faith still retained some of that free-spiritedness. It was another thing Lindsey envied about her. No matter what life threw at her, she seemed to take it in her stride.

An hour and a half later, they were sprawled out over the couch, the coffee table littered with empty takeout boxes. They had started drinking while waiting for the food to arrive, and Lindsey was starting to feel it.

Faith refilled her glass, then looked at Lindsey's empty one. "Want some more?"

"If I didn't know better, I'd think you're trying to get me drunk," Lindsey said. It was already too late for that.

"I just want to see you have some fun," Faith said, drawing out her words like she always did after a few drinks. "You've been so mopey lately."

"Yeah, well everything sucks right now."

"What's the matter?" Faith asked. "Other than getting kicked out of your moldy apartment, that is."

"It's mostly work. Spending forty hours a week stuck in a cubicle trying to sell people something they don't need? It's so soul-destroying."

"Why don't you find another job?" Faith asked. "Something you actually like?"

"I wish I could. I don't have any real skills."

"You were one of the best artists in our class. I think it's safe to say you've got skills."

"Fine, I don't have any useful skills," Lindsey said. "Art doesn't pay the bills. Not unless you're some combination of brilliant and extremely lucky."

"You could try nannying. It wasn't what I thought I'd be doing after college either, but it's fun. And you can make lots of money once you have some experience."

"I'm not good with kids. I wouldn't know what to do."

Faith pursed her lips in thought. "There are other ways to make money, you know." She lowered her voice. "Ways other than jobs."

Lindsey sat upright. "What do you mean?"

"It's probably easier if I show you." Faith stood up. "I'm going to go grab my laptop. I'll be right back." She headed to her bedroom, swaying as she walked.

Lindsey stared at the pitcher on the table. She'd already had far too much to drink. But she was tired of being a responsible adult. She was tired of constantly worrying about work, and money, and debt. All she wanted was to pretend that she was still the carefree young woman she'd been just a year or two ago.

And most of all, she wanted to forget about the fact that she was now living a life that would have made her younger self so disappointed in her.

Lindsey refilled her glass and started gulping her drink down. Just as she finished it off, Faith returned to the living room and sat down next to her.

"I should warn you," Faith said, typing a web address into her browser. "This is a little unconventional."

"I don't care," Lindsey said. "Show me."

That was where her memory of that night ended.

CHAPTER TWO

After a long day at work, Lindsey returned to Faith's apartment. She'd stayed back late for yet another meeting with her boss about her performance. It hadn't improved. Lindsey couldn't help but wonder if she was subconsciously sabotaging herself so that she'd be fired.

She sat down on the couch. She could worry about that tomorrow. Lindsey grabbed her laptop from the coffee table and opened it up. Some mindless TV was just what she needed. Lindsey found a show she was midway through binge-watching and pressed play.

Her phone buzzed. A message from Faith, telling Lindsey that she was at the grocery store and would be home soon. Lindsey flicked through her phone, only half watching the show playing on her laptop screen. Her email inbox was full of unread messages. She scrolled through them, deleting most of the emails without opening them.

A particular email caught her eye. The subject line read: *Welcome to thesugarbowl.com.*

That had to be spam. But the name of the website jogged something in Lindsey's memory. She opened the email.

Congratulations. Your application to join The Sugar Bowl has been accepted. Click here to view your profile.

What was this? Lindsey didn't remember signing up for anything like it. She clicked the link. It took her to a profile page on what looked like a dating website. *Her* profile page, complete with photos.

And underneath her profile picture were the words "Sugar Baby looking for arrangement."

What the hell? Suddenly, snippets of Friday night started coming back to her. Lindsey groaned. She'd been right in thinking that getting drunk with Faith could only lead to disaster. Lindsey still didn't remember the details, but maybe her friend did. She dialed Faith's number.

Faith answered in her usual cheery voice. "What's up, Lindsey?"

"Why am I signed up for a sugar baby website?" Lindsey asked.

"Oh yeah, I forgot all about that. Does this mean you got accepted?"

"Apparently. But I don't remember any of this."

"Nothing?" Faith asked. "Wow. Well, you did drink a lot. But you seemed really keen on the idea at the time. All I did was help you set up your profile."

Lindsey shook her head. "This is crazy. I should just delete my profile."

"What? You can't! That website is really hard to get onto, especially if you're a woman. There are just too many women who want to be sugar babies. Plus, they screen everyone really carefully."

"How do you even know all this?" Lindsey asked.

"That friend of mine from freshman year?" Faith said. "I guess you don't remember that conversation either?"

"Nope."

"Look, I have to go, but I'll be home in ten minutes. We can talk about this then. Whatever you do, do *not* delete your profile."

"Fine," Lindsey said.

"I'll see you soon."

Lindsey hung up and placed her phone down. She would humor her friend. She wasn't actually considering becoming a sugar baby. Although, she only had a basic idea of what being a sugar baby involved. And it couldn't hurt to have a look at the website. To take a peek at this world of money, and glamour, and romance.

Abandoning her TV show, Lindsey opened up the Sugar Bowl website on her laptop and logged into her profile. A few pictures of her from social media were at the top, and all her information, from her age to her height, was listed underneath. She'd written a short biography too. Lindsey had to admit, she and Faith had done a good job. The profile made Lindsey sound much more interesting than she was in real life. And much more alluring.

There was a red envelope symbol at the top of the screen with the number 23 written next to it. Did Lindsey have 23 messages already? She opened up her inbox and went through the messages one by one.

The first was from a man who listed himself as forty, but he was clearly at least sixty. And his message? It was polite and respectful at first, but then he openly admitted to having a wife and said he was looking for someone 'discreet.'

Lindsey shuddered and moved on to the next message. It was much the same, minus the wife. But it was loaded with hints about the man's sexual prowess. *No thanks.*

The rest of the messages were no better. Several of the men were just looking for sex. A few of them seemed genuine, but they were all old enough to be her grandfather.

Finally, she reached the last message. It was from someone named Camilla.

A woman? Lindsey tapped the thumbnail to view Camilla's profile. There was only one photo of her. It showed a gorgeous long-haired brunette with an inviting smile, bright hazel eyes, and an air of unwavering confidence that Lindsey could feel through the screen.

Lindsey scanned Camilla's profile. She was 39 years old, and her biography was concise and detailed. She was a businesswoman, who liked wine, architecture, and art. And nothing on her profile suggested she was after sex.

Lindsey frowned. Why was she even getting messages from a woman? Any good dating site would have the option to choose gender preferences. And Lindsey was as straight as they came.

Lindsey heard the sound of a key in the front door. A moment later, Faith entered the apartment juggling a few bags of groceries.

"Hey, Lindsey." She walked over to the couch and peered over Lindsey's shoulder. "Is that the Sugar Bowl? Did you get any bites yet?"

"I got a few messages," Lindsey replied.

"Oh? Does this mean you're not going to delete your profile?"

"I don't know. I mean, I'm not against the idea, but I don't know about the 'sleeping with someone for money' part."

Lindsey wasn't a prude when it came to sex. In fact, she was pretty adventurous. But even for her, this was a little too far. Maybe if she was actually attracted to the guy, it would be a different story. But judging by the caliber of men on the site, that wasn't going to happen.

"Being a sugar baby isn't about sex." Faith placed the grocery bags on the coffee table and perched on the arm of the couch. "It's about providing a girlfriend experience. Sometimes that involves sex, but sometimes it doesn't."

"And how do you know so much about this again?" Lindsey asked.

"I already told you, that girl I had a few classes with in freshman year. She started sugaring while she was still in art school. She ended up finding some rich guy who has been paying for all her living expenses for years now."

"Huh," Lindsey said. "He pays for everything?"

"Yep."

"And it's really not about sex?"

"Nope," Faith replied. "Apparently, the guy just likes having the company of a hot young woman. Whether there's sex involved or not, what these men are looking for is all the good parts of having a girlfriend without any of the bad parts. In return, they give their sugar baby gifts. They can be fancy dinners, designer clothes, expensive phones, or even just cash. Some of them give their sugar baby a monthly allowance or help them out with bills."

"That sounds like a pretty sweet deal," Lindsey said.

"Yep. I considered it myself after I graduated and couldn't find a job. Then the Yangs hired me full-time, so I didn't need to worry about money anymore."

"Hmm…" Lindsey glanced at her laptop again. Camilla's profile was still open. "We must have made a mistake setting up my account. My profile seems to be set to men and women."

"That wasn't a mistake." Faith grinned. "I talked you into ticking both boxes. It gives you more options."

"And how is that supposed to work?" Lindsey asked. "Last time I checked, I'm not interested in women. Not all of us are as enlightened as you and don't care about the gender of who we date."

"What about all those girls you made out with in college?" Faith teased.

"That doesn't count. I made out with everyone in college." It was true. But she'd never gone further than a kiss with another woman. She'd never felt any attraction to them.

"Wait, have you been getting messages from women?" Faith asked. "It's rare to find women who are looking for sugar babies."

"I got one message from a woman. Here." Lindsey turned her screen toward Faith. "She actually seems interesting."

"Wow," Faith said. "What a babe. And she's only 39. She messaged you?"

Lindsey nodded.

Faith pointed to a number on the screen. "The two of you are a 97% match. You're insanely compatible."

"How do they know that?"

"Remember all those questions we had to answer for the application?"

Lindsey shrugged.

"Right," Faith said. "You were drunk. They ask everyone a bunch of questions and then use algorithms to calculate how compatible two people are based on their answers. 97% is off the charts."

"Unfortunately, there's one problem with that," Lindsey said. "She's a woman. I don't like women. That's pretty important when it comes to compatibility."

"That might not matter in this case. By the looks of her profile, this woman isn't looking for sex. Maybe she just wants the company."

"Maybe." That could be fun. Going on fancy dates with some rich lady and getting paid to do it. "Either way, I'd be pretending to be interested in someone for their money. Isn't that a little predatory?"

"It's not like the other person isn't getting anything out of the deal," Faith said. "They're pretending too. It's not to say that the relationships can't be genuine. But do you really think these 21-year-old girls are attracted to their 60-year-old sugar daddies? Do you think they'd be with them if money wasn't involved? The sugar daddies—the mamas—they all know the score."

"Hmm." Lindsey chewed her lip. "I have to think about all this."

"Let me know if you have any more questions. I can even put you in touch with that friend of mine if you'd like." Faith got up and picked up the grocery bags from the table. "I'm going to put these away and have a shower. I've been chasing kids around all day."

As Faith left the room, Lindsey went over everything Faith had told her in her head. Maybe it wasn't such a crazy idea. The old Lindsey would have jumped at the chance to do something like this. She would have loved to be taken out and spoiled by some rich suitor in exchange for being their pretend girlfriend. The old Lindsey wouldn't have even cared if that suitor was a woman.

But that adventurous, carefree college kid was long gone, replaced by Lindsey the insurance saleswoman.

Maybe Lindsey couldn't afford to be as carefree as she used to be. But this could really help with her money problems. Lindsey turned back to her laptop. It was still open on Camilla's profile. Camilla seemed much more interesting than all the men who had messaged her, and Lindsey hadn't even read Camilla's message yet.

She went back to her inbox and opened the woman's message up. It was surprisingly short. All the other messages she'd been sent were page-long explanations of what the sender wanted from Lindsey. But this one was just a single sentence.

I'd love to take you out on a date.

That was it? It seemed presumptuous. Camilla hadn't asked Lindsey if she'd like to go on a date. She'd simply stated what she wanted. But there was something to be said for being direct.

Lindsey returned to the woman's profile. As she scrolled through it, her eyes landed on something at the bottom of Camilla's bio. She had missed it last time. It was a single word, on a line all on its own.

Dominant.

Lindsey's heart jumped. Camilla hadn't elaborated, but

she didn't have to. Lindsey had already detected some hint of it in the way Camilla held herself in her profile photo. This woman was a Dominant, with a capital D. Lindsey had dabbled enough in BDSM that she knew exactly what that meant.

And Lindsey was intrigued.

She brought up Camilla's message again. Her hands hovered above the keyboard. There was no harm in going on one date with her. If Lindsey had any reservations after meeting her, she could call everything off.

She thought for a moment, then typed out a response.

I'm free on Saturday night. Does that work for you?

Lindsey hit send and closed her laptop. It was done. At once, all sorts of doubts came to her. Had she been too forward? Had suggesting a Saturday night been a bad idea? Night meant dinner, drinks, or dancing. Should she have suggested something casual like coffee instead? But coffee barely counted as a date. Could this really be called a date?

It didn't matter. It was already done. Lindsey got up and shoved her laptop in her suitcase. She had to stop obsessing about this.

A few minutes later, her phone buzzed. She picked it up. It was an email from thesugarbowl.com containing a message from Camilla.

Saturday night is perfect. Let's have drinks at 8 p.m.

Before Lindsey could stop herself, she sent off a reply.

It's a date.

She set down her phone and sank down onto the couch. What had she done?

CHAPTER THREE

"You look like a nun," Faith said.

Lindsey stared at herself in Faith's bedroom mirror. Her long reddish hair was pulled back, and she'd spent plenty of time getting her makeup right, however, the black, knee-length dress she wore was pretty conservative. "The place we're going to for drinks is really classy. I don't want to look out of place."

"That doesn't mean you can't show a little skin. Don't you have anything sexier?"

Lindsey looked at the suitcase she'd dragged into Faith's room. "Most of my clothes are in storage. I didn't think I'd be going on a fancy date anytime soon."

"I have just the thing." Faith leaped up from the bed and started to go through her closet. "Where did I put it?"

Lindsey pulled off the dress, careful not to smudge her makeup, and added it to the pile of rejected outfits on Faith's bed. She couldn't remember the last time she'd dressed up like this. And she couldn't remember the last time she'd been this excited about anything, let alone a date.

Not that it was a real date. But even though it was pretend, a romantic night out at an upscale lounge sounded like the perfect escape from her dreary life.

"Found it!" Faith held up a black and silver patterned dress. "This. This is perfect."

"That's… short." Although Lindsey and Faith were the same size, Faith was much shorter. And the dress didn't even go down to Faith's knees.

"That's why I picked it. One look at you in this dress, and you'll have Camilla giving you whatever you ask for. Money, fancy clothes, a car."

Lindsey rolled her eyes and took the dress from Faith. "I'm not going to ask Camilla for money. I'm just going to meet her." She slipped the dress over her head.

"Well, you have to talk about the financial side of things, at least. You don't want to go on a bunch of dates only to find that your sugar mama isn't going to give you any sugar."

Lindsey looked in the mirror. The dress was exactly as short on her as she expected it to be. But it covered her up everywhere else. And it did look pretty classy.

"See?" Faith said. "It's perfect."

Lindsey turned in the mirror. "I sure hope so."

"You seem nervous."

"Well yeah. I mean I've never done anything like this before."

"Just treat it like any other date," Faith said. "Well, a date with someone you're really trying to impress. Flirt, compliment her, laugh at her jokes. Show an interest in her life."

"I can do that." Lindsey picked up her phone and looked at the time. "I should get going."

"Okay. Don't forget to check in with me when you get there. Just so I know you're okay and that this woman isn't some creep."

"I doubt Camilla is a creep."

"You never know," Faith said. "And if anything happens, and you need rescuing, call me."

"Is there anything else, Mom?" Lindsey asked.

Faith stuck out her tongue. "I'm just looking out for you. I know you weren't sure about this, so if you start to feel uncomfortable, get out of there."

"I will, I promise. And I don't feel weird about this anymore. I'm actually pretty excited." Lindsey took one last look in the mirror and smoothed down her dress. "Wish me luck."

Lindsey's ride pulled up to the club where she was meeting Camilla. The Lounge was an exclusive upmarket bar that catered to the city's wealthy. As Lindsey stepped out onto the sidewalk, she wondered if she'd even be able to get inside. Then she spotted Camilla waiting for her out front.

The woman was even more beautiful in person than in her photos. Her chocolate brown hair was dead straight, and she had the kind of curves that would make a fifties pinup model jealous. Her black dress, which was short and tight but had long sleeves, flattered every inch of her. She was shorter than Lindsey, even in heels, but she somehow managed to look like she stood above everyone else around her. Lindsey knew from Camilla's profile that she was 39, but Lindsey would have pegged her for a bit younger. Either way, she certainly looked older than Lindsey.

Suddenly, Lindsey felt like a high schooler.

As Lindsey stood on the sidewalk examining Camilla, the woman turned her way and gave her a warm smile.

Lindsey collected herself. *Here goes nothing.* She strode over to the other woman.

"Camilla," she said. "Hi."

"You must be Lindsey. It's a pleasure to meet you." Camilla's voice was melodious and clear, and she had a refined way of speaking. "Let's go inside."

Lindsey glanced at the line at the entrance of the bar. They were going to be waiting for a while. But Camilla simply walked to the door and gave a brief nod to security, who stepped aside without hesitation.

They entered the club. It was even more luxurious than Lindsey expected. Glittering lights. Gold accents on everything. Plush seating. Despite the line outside, the dimly lit club wasn't full. Men and women lounged about, all dressed in suits and dresses. The music was loud, but not so loud that they'd have to shout to talk. It was the perfect place to take a date if you wanted to impress them.

And Lindsey was impressed.

Camilla led her to a small corner booth. "After you."

Lindsey took a seat. The booth was only big enough for two. Camilla slid in after her and sat down so that they were half facing each other, half next to each other.

Camilla looked around the bar. "I haven't been here for a while. I have to say, it's a lot tackier than I remember." She brushed some invisible dust off the table in front of her.

Lindsey didn't know what Camilla was talking about.

This place was classier than anywhere Lindsey had ever been.

A waitress came over to take their orders. Camilla ordered a cocktail, so Lindsey did the same.

"We'll have the truffle fries too," Camilla said. She turned back to Lindsey. "I hope you're hungry. I don't usually eat this kind of food, but the truffle fries are to die for."

What kind of person doesn't eat fries? Lindsey looked around. She couldn't help but feel out of her element. And not just because of the fancy bar. Camilla herself looked like she was too good even for a place like this. She was sitting next to Lindsey with perfect posture like she was having dinner with the queen.

"Is everything okay?" Camilla asked.

"Yeah," Lindsey said. "I'm just a bit nervous. I'm still new to this." She meant the sugar baby part, not the 'going on a date with a woman' part.

"I know it can be nerve-wracking at first. It's easiest to think of it as the two of us getting to know each other. No pressure, and no obligations."

"Okay." Lindsey remembered Faith's advice. *Flirt. Show an interest in her.* Lindsey was too nervous to flirt. Instead, she opted for the latter. "So, what do you do for work?" It wasn't a very exciting topic, but it was all she could think of.

"I run my family's company," Camilla said.

"Wow." Not her family's business. Her family's *company.* "That sounds like a lot of work."

"It takes up almost all my time and energy. I mostly work from home for efficiency's sake, which helps. But I enjoy it. It's been in my family for generations and I inherited the company from my parents years ago. I've managed to build on their successes since then."

"What is it that your company does, exactly?" Lindsey asked.

"Oh, a little of everything. You'd find it all dreadfully boring."

The waitress returned with their drinks, along with a large plate of truffle fries

Camilla took a sip of her cocktail. "Well, at least they still make decent drinks. Here." She pushed the plate of fries toward Lindsey. "Try some."

"Thanks." Lindsey grabbed a few and nibbled on them. They were good.

"How about you?" Camilla said. "What do you do?"

"Well, at the moment I work at a call center selling overpriced insurance to people who don't need it."

"That sounds delightful," Camilla said dryly.

"It's pretty depressing," Lindsey said. "But it pays the bills, and I really need the money." *Crap.* Now she sounded like she was begging Camilla for money. "Sorry, I didn't mean to bring money up."

"Oh, it's fine. I'm not the type to delude myself that some beautiful young woman is actually interested in me and not my money." Camilla looked Lindsey up and down. "All my charms aside, I'm old enough to be your mother."

"You'd have been a pretty young mother."

"Trying to flatter me, are you?"

Lindsey shrugged. "It's true."

More small talk followed, and Lindsey began to relax. No doubt, the cocktail helped. Soon, they were onto their second round of drinks.

"So," Camilla asked. "What are you looking for in an arrangement?"

"Uh, I'm not sure," Lindsey said.

"You really are new to this. Most women have a whole speech ready."

"Actually, you're the only person I've met up with."

"I'm flattered," Camilla said. "But a word of advice? Don't be afraid to speak up about your needs, or you'll get taken advantage of."

Lindsey nodded.

"So, what is it you're after? Someone who will take you out to fancy dinners? Help to pay off your student loans?" Camilla took a sip of her cocktail. "Money for a set of double D's?"

Lindsey almost choked on her fries. "You mean a boob job?"

"It wouldn't be the first time."

"No, that's not what I want. I guess I'd like some help paying off my medical debt. I was in a car accident a year ago, and I ended up with a whole heap of bills that weren't covered by insurance. Plus, my apartment building has been shut down because it's a health hazard, so I need a new place to live, but I can't find anything within my budget. I'm sleeping on my best friends couch for now, but I can't stay there forever. So, help with my living expenses would be great too."

"That's a very sensible answer," Camilla said. "What made you decide to try sugaring?"

"Well, Faith—the friend I'm living with—told me about it, and it seemed like it could be a fun solution to my problems," Lindsey said. "Plus, I've been in a bit of a rut lately. I wanted to do something exciting."

"And? Are you finding this exciting so far?"

A smile tugged at Lindsey's lips. "I am." She'd been worried she'd have to fake interest in Camilla. But Lindsey liked her. "Did someone really ask you for money for a boob job?"

Camilla nodded. "A young woman with aspirations of being an actress. Lovely, but a terrible conversationalist. I've had more interesting chats with my ninety-year-old groundskeeper about the lawn."

Lindsey wasn't at all surprised that Camilla had a groundskeeper.

"Most of the women I've met through the Sugar Bowl have been the same," Camilla said. "Nice, but we didn't click. Don't get me wrong, I'm under no illusions about these types of arrangements. Nonetheless, if we're going to be spending time together, we need to be able to connect on some level."

Lindsey nodded. But there was a question at the back of her mind. "Why did you sign up for the Sugar Bowl? It's not like you'd have any trouble finding a real girlfriend."

"You think I don't know that?" Camilla asked.

"I didn't mean-"

"To put it simply, I'm a busy woman. Relationships are hard work. And they're messy. The way I see it is, I can go out on the dating scene and try to find someone who fits my strict ideas about what I'm looking for in a relationship. Or I can find a beautiful young woman who will give me exactly what I need, in exchange for being spoiled rotten."

Lindsey remembered all the men who had sent her

messages filled with innuendo. "What is it that you need, exactly?"

Camilla raised an eyebrow. "Darling," she said, drawing out the 'a.' "If I wanted sex, I would have hired an escort. What I want is a companion of sorts. A girlfriend without all the strings and baggage that normally comes with one. A relationship on my terms, that fulfills certain requirements."

Lindsey sipped her drink and glanced up at Camilla. "What kind of requirements?"

"You suddenly have a lot of questions."

"We're supposed to be getting to know each other, aren't we?"

Camilla sat back and crossed her arms. "If you must know, I like to take charge in a relationship. And I don't just mean in bed. I like control. I like things done a certain way. I like my routines. A lot of women have a problem with that. More than one ex-girlfriend of mine has called me a control freak."

"I don't see anything wrong with that," Lindsey said. "And I don't mind being on the other end. Of giving up control. It's nice, sometimes, to be told what to do. To have someone else make decisions for you. It can be freeing, not to have to worry about the little things."

Lindsey paused, suddenly realizing she was revealing her deepest desires to a woman she'd just met. And Camilla was watching her with an interest that made Lindsey's skin prickle.

"It makes everything simple, that's all," Lindsey said. "My exes thought it was weird too. The last guy I dated thought that 'taking charge' meant being a controlling jerk. I've never broken up with someone so fast."

"You date men *and* women, then?" Camilla asked.

Lindsey froze. She'd gotten so comfortable with Camilla that she'd forgotten about the small matter of her lack of interest in women. But she couldn't bring herself to outright lie about it.

"It's not a problem, of course," Camilla said hurriedly. "I'm not one of those people who think bisexual women are just looking for a vacation from men. I just ask because I find it very hard to believe you're still on the market when you have the pick of all the men on the site. There are so many more of them than women. You're spoiled for choice. And I know someone like you has gotten dozens of messages."

That was a close call. "I have gotten a lot of messages," Lindsey said. "But none of the men who sent them appealed to me. Not like you did." That was the truth.

"Oh? And what exactly appealed to you about me?"

"What can I say?" Lindsey leaned in a little closer. She was feeling daring. "You're gorgeous, for starters. And your profile was interesting. It drew me to you. And your message was very direct. I liked that." She paused. She didn't want to seem like she was fawning.

"Oh, don't stop," Camilla said. "I was enjoying hearing all the wonderful things about me."

Lindsey bit her lip. "And I saw that we have something in common."

"Oh?" Camilla tilted her head to the side slightly. "Are you referring to a love of wine?"

Lindsey shook her head.

Camilla paused. "I take it you're not referring to my interest in classic architecture?"

"Nope."

"Then what is it?" The look in Camilla's hazel eyes made it clear that she already knew the answer.

For a second, Lindsey's words caught in her throat. "You're a dominant."

Camilla's expression didn't change. "And you're a submissive."

"Yes," Lindsey replied, even though it wasn't a question.

A cat-like smile spread across Camilla's face. "Well, this just got a lot more interesting."

A waiter came over to ask if they needed anything. Camilla ordered them both another drink. They sat in silence as the waiter cleared away their empty glasses.

As soon as he was gone, Camilla spoke. "All this time, you knew I was a dominant, yet you still made me tell you about what I require from a relationship?" Her voice dropped to a firm, smoky whisper. "That was very naughty of you."

Heat rushed to Lindsey's cheeks.

Camilla chuckled softly. "Is that all it takes to make you squirm? You really are a submissive."

"Well, I haven't had a lot of experience," Lindsey said. "I wish I had more. But the scene, the clubs, the rules—it's all really intimidating."

"I understand. The scene isn't very beginner friendly sometimes."

Camilla reached out and placed a sympathetic hand on Lindsey's. The fleeting touch seemed to linger on her skin even after Camilla pulled away.

"You were right," Camilla said. "We do have a lot in common."

From then on, the conversation flowed much more freely. It was easy with Camilla. She was warm and witty, and made Lindsey feel at ease. And whenever Camilla made a suggestive comment, Lindsey couldn't help but flirt back.

After they reached the end of their second serving of fries and countless drinks, Camilla sat back in her chair and studied Lindsey.

"I like you, Lindsey. You're the first woman I've met on the Sugar Bowl who doesn't seem like you're working from a script. You're refreshingly honest."

"Good company brings that out in me," Lindsey said. Her cheeks felt warm. "The cocktails help."

A large group of drunk men blustered by their table. A couple of them turned their heads to stare at Camilla and Lindsey as they passed.

Camilla gave them a dark glare until they were out of view. "Clearly, this place is being taken over by riff-raff." She looked at her watch. "It's getting late. I live a little outside the city, so I should head home. Let's get going."

"Sure." Lindsey was surprised by how much time had passed.

Camilla paid off their tab, which Lindsey was sure was extravagant, and the two of them headed outside.

"I'll call a car to take you home." Camilla pulled out her phone. "On me, of course."

"You don't have to," Lindsey said.

"But I want to. I have to call one for myself too." Without waiting for a response, she tapped the screen of her phone a few times and tucked it back into her purse. "Done. They should be here in a few minutes."

The two of them walked a short distance down the

street, away from the entrance to the bar. The night air was cool on Lindsey's skin.

Lindsey broke the silence. "This was… nice."

"It was," Camilla said. "I've certainly enjoyed this more than all my recent dates. Probably because they were all with women who were so painfully straight that they couldn't keep up the illusion. If this is going to be one big charade, the least everyone could do is be convincing about it."

Right. Lindsey couldn't tell Camilla that she was just like all of those other straight women. She was in too deep now.

"What is it?" Camilla asked. "I find it hard to believe you've suddenly gotten shy."

"It's just, I, actually… I've never been with a woman before," Lindsey blurted out. "On a date, I mean." That much was true.

"Oh?"

"But I've kissed one," she added. "Well, more than one."

Camilla's lips curled up. "Would you like to kiss another one?"

Lindsey barely even hesitated. She'd already gone this far. If she was going to do something crazy, she might as well go all the way. "Yes," she said. "I would."

Camilla took Lindsey's chin in her fingers and leaned in close. "Then kiss me."

Lindsey's pulse raced. Camilla's smooth, commanding voice resonated deep into her body, compelling her to do as Camilla told her.

Closing her eyes, Lindsey kissed Camilla. It was a brief touch of the lips, nothing more. But it seemed to go on and on. For a moment, Lindsey forgot herself, as Camilla's lips took over all her awareness.

Camilla pulled back. "Your car is here."

Lindsey opened her eyes. A black car had pulled up beside them.

Camilla opened the door for her. "I'll send you a little something for tonight?"

Did she mean money? "You don't have to," Lindsey said.

"Once again, I want to, so I'm going to. You really haven't done this before, have you?"

"It just feels weird, getting paid for something like this."

"I'm not paying you," Camilla said. "It's a gift. Accept it."

"Okay. Thank you." Lindsey slid into the backseat of the car. "Goodnight."

"Goodnight, Lindsey. I'll talk to you soon."

CHAPTER FOUR

Lindsey was in Faith's living room on Sunday afternoon when Faith returned home from work. They hadn't seen each other since before Lindsey left to meet Camilla the night before.

Faith walked over to the couch, lifted Lindsey's legs up and sat down next to her. "Tell me all about your date."

Lindsey stretched her legs across Faith's lap. "I already told you about it last night." Faith had insisted Lindsey check in afterward.

"Yes, but you didn't tell me the details."

Sighing, Lindsey told Faith everything, from the moment she stepped out of the cab, all the way to when she and Camilla left the bar. "And then, we kissed."

"Whoa, hold on," Faith said. "You and Camilla kissed? And you're only telling me this now?"

Lindsey shrugged. "I was feeling kinda weird about it. Not because it was bad or anything. It was… nice."

"Ooh, do I detect a crush?"

"It was just a kiss. No matter how amazing Camilla is, she doesn't have the right equipment."

"This may come as a shock to you, but when it comes to women who are into women, a lack of equipment is rarely a problem."

Lindsey picked up a cushion and threw it at Faith, who batted it away harmlessly.

"Did you talk about money, at least?" Faith asked.

"Not directly. We talked about what we both wanted from an arrangement. And she sent me some money through the Sugar Bowl website after the date. A gift, she called it."

"How much money?"

"Three hundred dollars," Lindsey replied.

"Seriously?"

Lindsey nodded. "I was blown away too. Three hundred dollars just to spend a few hours with someone in a nice bar? Even if Camilla hadn't given me money in the end, I wouldn't have considered it a waste of time. We get along really well."

And Lindsey couldn't help but feel flattered. It wasn't every day Lindsey met a gorgeous dominant who was interested in her.

"See," Faith said. "The website's algorithm was right about the two of you being a good match."

Lindsey crossed her legs in Faith's lap. "We do have a few things in common."

"Like what?"

"Well, she likes art." The two of them had discussed art, but Lindsey hadn't mentioned that she was an artist. It wasn't like she'd ever be a real one. "And, she's a Domme."

Lindsey watched her friend's face for a reaction. She'd told Faith about her unconventional tastes one night when they'd been drinking together. Faith hadn't been fazed, but she didn't seem to understand it either.

"Weren't you just saying you're not into women?" Faith asked. "And now you're excited because Camilla likes kinky sex?"

"BDSM isn't about sex," Lindsey said. "Sure, there's usually a sexual element to it, but it's about so much more than that."

"Right." The skepticism on Faith's face grew.

"I know it doesn't look that way from the outside, but-" How could Lindsey explain the magnetic appeal of a Domme to Faith? There were certain things that Faith seemed completely naive about, and this was one of them. "A lot of people view it as something like a hobby or a lifestyle. It's an interest we're both passionate about, like hiking or something." It wasn't quite the same, but it was the only comparison she could think of.

"It's definitely more interesting than hiking," Faith said.

"Well, Domme or not, woman or not, I want to see her again," Lindsey said. "There's something about her that... I just can't describe it. She's so captivating."

"It's nice to see you happy about something. Does this mean the two of you are going to go out again?"

"We don't have anything planned, but she said we'd talk soon before we parted ways on Friday night. I haven't heard from her yet, but she seemed interested in going out again." Lindsey had been checking her phone compulsively.

"That's great," Faith said. "Aren't you glad you listened to me and didn't delete your profile?"

"I am," Lindsey admitted.

"When your sugar mama starts buying you fancy clothes, you better let me borrow them."

"It's a deal."

As if on cue, Lindsey's phone rang.

Faith leaned over and peered at her screen. "It's her! Hurry up and answer it."

Lindsey stood up. "I will. In private."

"You're no fun," Faith said.

Lindsey walked into the bathroom and shut the door behind her. "Hi, Camilla."

"Lindsey." Camilla's sweet voice came through the line. "I hope I'm not interrupting anything."

"No, it's fine." Lindsey sat down on the edge of the bathtub. "I'm just hanging out with Faith in her apartment."

"The friend who convinced you to sign up for the Sugar Bowl? I should thank her."

"God, no. Faith would love that. She's been so smug and happy about the fact that I went on a date with someone."

"And how do *you* feel about said date?" Camilla asked.

"I'm pretty happy about it too," Lindsey replied. "I had a great time."

"So did I. I'd love to take you out again."

"I'd like that."

"Next Saturday," Camilla said. "We'll go to dinner."

"Okay. I can't wait." Lindsey hesitated. "And thanks for the gift." She wasn't sure if it was more impolite to mention it or to not thank her for it.

"My pleasure. I do enjoy having someone to spoil. It isn't quite enough money for a boob job, but I hope it'll help with those bills of yours."

Lindsey smiled. "It will. I'll see you on Saturday."

She hung up and let out a breath. She was really doing this. Lindsey got up, opened the bathroom door, and almost walked right into Faith.

"So," Faith said. "What did Camilla say?"

"Were you listening the whole time?" Lindsey asked.

"I was trying to, but I couldn't hear anything through this stupid door." Faith put her hands on her hips. "Well?"

"Well, we're going out again on Saturday. She's taking me to dinner."

"That's great," Faith said. "You're going to need something to wear."

CHAPTER FIVE

"I hope you left room for dessert," Camilla said. "I have a sweet tooth, and this place does an amazing crème brûlée. The servings are enormous, so we'll have to share."

"Sure," Lindsey said.

The night was going well. Just like their last date, Camilla had taken Lindsey somewhere fancier than she'd ever be able to afford herself. And, like their last date, Lindsey had started out a bundle of nerves, but Camilla had made her feel at ease. Dinner had simply flown by.

There had been a minor incident when Camilla had sent back a perfectly good plate of scallops because they 'tasted like something from the bottom of a supermarket freezer.' Lindsey wondered if Camilla had ever eaten anything from a supermarket freezer before. Or if she'd even set foot in a supermarket.

"They also do an amazing tiramisu," Camilla said. "Which do you prefer?"

"I don't mind," Lindsey replied. "Whatever you want."

"Whatever I want? What if I wanted you to kneel by my feet while I fed you dessert?"

An image sprung up in Lindsey's mind. Of herself, kneeling on the floor next to Camilla's chair in the middle of the restaurant in front of everyone.

She looked Camilla in the eye. "I would do it."

"You really would, wouldn't you?"

"I would if you told me to."

"That's right. You like being told what to do."

Camilla folded her arms across her chest and leaned back, examining Lindsey silently. Lindsey shifted in her seat.

"Have I told you about where I live?" Camilla asked suddenly. "Robinson Estate?"

"No," Lindsey replied.

"It's an hour outside the city. The grounds are lovely. It's almost like living in the countryside. The estate dates back to the 1700s, but the manor itself has been renovated so many times that it's basically brand new. It spans two floors, and there are over 100 rooms. And it's equipped with every luxury imaginable."

"That sounds incredible." Lindsey waited for Camilla to continue. It looked like she had more to say, but she seemed to be thinking deeply.

Finally, Camilla folded her hands in front of her. "I have a proposal for you. It's unconventional, but it could be a solution to some of your problems."

"What is it?" Lindsey asked.

"Come live with me," Camilla said. "Move into my manor for three months. In exchange, I'll give you enough money to pay off all your medical bills and more."

Lindsey blinked. Had she heard that right? "That's... my medical bills. They're a lot."

"How much?"

Lindsey told her.

"I'll give you triple that," Camilla said.

Lindsey's jaw dropped. "Seriously?"

Camilla nodded. "I'll give you a generous weekly allowance too, just so you don't feel like you're being held hostage."

"No way," Lindsey said. "That's too much."

"Please, I have handbags that cost more than that."

Lindsey didn't know if Camilla was exaggerating about the handbags. What she was offering was enough money to pay off all Lindsey's medical bills, as well as a big chunk of her student loans from her useless fine arts degree. And she wouldn't have to worry about money for a while. She could quit her job at the call center and take her time looking for something better after three months was up.

"On top of that, my manor will be your home for three months," Camilla said. "I'll provide you with everything you could ever want. Luxury beyond your wildest dreams."

Lindsey pictured it all in her head. Would there be even more fancy dinners? Expensive clothes? Parties? Servants? It all seemed too good to be true.

Lindsey took a step back. "What do you want in return?" she asked. "What do you want me to be for you?"

"That's up to you," Camilla said. "I'd be fine with you being nothing more than my companion. It gets boring sometimes, living in that enormous house with no one else around except for the help. I'd appreciate the company, and

I think you can agree that we get along well. But there are other options if you're interested."

"Like what?" Lindsey asked.

"You can be my temporary live-in girlfriend." Camilla paused. "Or, you can be my submissive."

Her submissive? Lindsey couldn't deny that the idea appealed to her. She'd never been anyone's submissive before. She had only seen glimpses of Camilla's dominant side, and she liked what she saw.

But still, Camilla was a woman. And that wasn't something Lindsey could ignore, could she?

"Is something the matter?" Camilla asked.

"It's just that…" Lindsey hesitated. "Like I said, I've never actually been with a woman before." She felt a twinge of guilt. She was avoiding the whole truth.

"I said from the start that I'm not after sex. Quite frankly, I can take it or leave it. And I would never pressure you in any way. I take consent and boundaries very seriously." Camilla fixed her eyes on Lindsey's. "What I want is something much more intimate than sex, and far more satisfying. A submissive who will be mine 24/7. Who will obey me, and defer to me, and serve me. Who will do as I say without question and thank me for it every single day."

Lindsey's skin flushed. On the surface, Camilla always appeared laid back, if not a bit stuck up. But it was becoming clear that behind her cool demeanor was someone who needed to maintain an iron grip on control.

And the thought excited Lindsey.

"Whatever you decide, this won't be a one-way agreement," Camilla said. "I have certain conditions, but we can negotiate something we're both comfortable with."

"Wow," Lindsey said. "This is just…"

"Crazy? I realize that. I'm not in the habit of asking sugar babies to move into my manor. I've never even had a sugar baby before. But when you mentioned your housing problems, the idea came to me. I think this arrangement could be beneficial to both of us."

This arrangement. Because that was all it was, in the end. Camilla knew that it was all pretend. And this offer was too good to pass up.

"If you're not interested, I won't be offended," Camilla said. "I'm open to a more conventional sugar baby arrangement."

"No," Lindsey said. "I'm interested. It's just, it's a lot. Can I think about it?"

"Of course. Take all the time you need."

Lindsey didn't want to take time. She wanted to say yes right now. But leaping into something like this was irresponsible.

A waiter approached their table. "Will you be having dessert?" he asked.

"Yes," Camilla said. "Let's see. The crème brûlée, or the tiramisu? I simply can't decide." She thought for a moment, then smiled.

"We'll have both. Life is too short. Why not live a little?"

By the time Lindsey returned to Faith's apartment, it was late, and Faith was already asleep. Lindsey wished her friend was awake. She wanted someone to talk to about Camilla's proposal.

She sat down at the kitchen table and placed her phone in front of her. She was still reeling from the kiss Camilla had given her when they parted. Lindsey liked kissing Camilla. She liked just being around Camilla. She wanted nothing more than to say yes to her.

But Camilla was practically a stranger. Although, after two dates, Lindsey was beginning to get a sense of what the woman was like. She could be warm and outgoing at times, sharp and cynical at others. And Camilla seemed very conscious of the fact that their arrangement was nothing more than just that.

So why not take Camilla up on her offer? Lindsey could just treat these three months like a job. She was selling her soul at the call center every day, so this would be an improvement. Not to mention that it would be a step up from her current life. Three months of luxury and romance, with a magnetic woman who wanted to spoil Lindsey in exchange for her submission.

It was strange. This past year, Lindsey had been a constant mess of anxiety and indecision, lost and directionless, but too afraid to take the slightest risk.

Right now? She had no doubts about what she wanted to do.

Lindsey picked up her phone and dialed Camilla's number.

Camilla answered after a few rings. "Hello, Lindsey. I wasn't expecting to hear from you so soon."

"Camilla," Lindsey said. "I was thinking. About your proposal."

"And?"

"And my answer is yes."

The other end of the line was silent.

"Which parts of my proposal are you referring to?" Camilla asked.

"All of it," Lindsey said. "Yes, I'll come live with you. Yes, I'll be your companion. Yes, I'll be your submissive. Yes to everything."

"I'm glad you decided to accept my offer. We can discuss the details over the next few days. Once we've come to an agreement, you can move in whenever you like."

"Okay," Lindsey said.

"And Lindsey?" Camilla asked.

"Yes?"

"From now on, you'll call me Mistress."

CHAPTER SIX

"This is crazy," Faith said from the kitchen. "You know that, right?"

"I know." Lindsey tossed a pair of jeans into her suitcase. "But I'm doing it anyway."

It was 8:30 a.m. Lindsey had a couple of hours before the car Camilla sent was due to pick her up. Fortunately, she'd been living out of a suitcase for the past few weeks, so she didn't have much to pack.

Faith sat down on the couch with a bowl of cereal. "How well do you even know Camilla? What kind of woman invites a stranger to come live with her? She could be a serial killer!"

"Camilla is not a serial killer," Lindsey said. "I trust her. And I feel like we have a connection. I wouldn't be doing this otherwise, no matter how much money was involved."

"Okay," Faith said. "But what I don't get is that a minute ago you were on the fence about even meeting her because she was a woman. And now you're going to be her live-in lover?"

"I'm not going to be her lover." Lindsey pulled her phone charger out of the wall and tossed it into her suitcase. "I'm going to be her submissive."

"Isn't that the same thing? Isn't the whole point of all that kinky stuff to get off?"

"Not really," Lindsey said. "There doesn't have to be sex involved. There doesn't even have to be anything physical involved. Fundamentally, it's about power. Giving it up. Taking it away. The way that makes you feel."

"So, you're going to be her slave?" Faith asked.

"That's not Camilla's style. All she wants is someone who will say 'yes, Mistress,' and will happily do whatever she asks of them."

Over the course of the past week, Lindsey and Camilla had discussed their expectations. Lindsey had quickly learned that Camilla wasn't the type of dominant who used force of any kind to keep her submissive in line. She simply expected her submissive to yield to her control without question.

Lindsey was more than happy to do so. It was what she loved the most about submission. It made everything simple. It freed her from all her worries and problems. And right now, she had a long list of problems. She wanted this more than anything. She needed it.

"I still don't get it," Faith said. "Why would you let someone control you?"

"I'm not letting her control me," Lindsey replied. "I'm *choosing* to give her control. There's a difference. And I'm only giving her control of some things."

Camilla had sent Lindsey a long, detailed questionnaire about all things BDSM to fill out. There were questions about her likes, her dislikes, her limits. And they were comprehensive, covering the obvious activities like bondage, as well as things that were more mundane. How would Lindsey feel about being called a pet name, or wearing her Mistresses collar 24/7? Would she like it if her Mistress chose what she wore every day? What she ate? There were plenty of things that Lindsey had vetoed. But there were even more that she enthusiastically agreed to.

"I'm not going to do anything with her that I'm not comfortable with. And she's made it clear that she's going to respect my boundaries." Lindsey zipped up her suitcase and sat down next to Faith. "Plus, I've been thinking about the sex side of things. It isn't completely off the table. I'm not opposed to sleeping with a woman."

Faith cocked her head to the side. "Could it be that Camilla has turned you to the queer side?"

"I'm just a little curious, that's all." And who better to explore with than Camilla? A thought occurred to Lindsey. "God, I don't know anything about sex with women. How would I even know what to do? What if I'm terrible at it?"

"It's all about communication," Faith said. "Just tell Camilla you've never had sex with a woman before."

"I already told her. I didn't mean to, but it was this whole awkward mess and now she thinks I'm bisexual but inexperienced with women."

"Did you tell her you were bi?"

"No, she kind of came to that conclusion herself. And I didn't correct her." Lindsey pushed her guilt aside. "It doesn't matter. Camilla herself said that this was all a big charade. I just have to keep it up for three months."

"Uh huh," Faith said.

"Don't get all judgmental on me now."

Faith held up her hands. "No judgment here. But I should get to work." She pulled Lindsey in for a hug. "I expect updates from the minute you arrive."

"Sure," Lindsey said.

"And be safe. Call me the moment Camilla shows any sign of wanting to tie you up and lock you in her dungeon." Faith grinned. "Although, by the sound of things, both of you would probably like that."

The drive to Robinson Estate was a long one. At least, it felt long to Lindsey. Ever since her car accident, lengthy drives made her nervous. But it was nothing she couldn't handle.

The car stopped in front of a large set of double gates, which opened slowly before them like magic. They had reached Camilla's estate. Lindsey rolled down the window and stuck her head out, staring at the sprawling grounds. She could only just see the manor itself in the distance, a large white building at the end of a long, winding driveway.

Finally, the car pulled up in front of the manor. The mansion looked even more impressive close-up. Lindsey got out of the car and stood staring at the house as the driver took her bags out of the trunk.

She scratched the back of her head. What was she supposed to do now? Knock on the door?

Moments later, the front door opened, and a short blonde woman came hurrying out. Her hair was pulled back in a bun, and her face wore a neutral expression. She was dressed in a navy-blue maid uniform, complete with a frilly white apron. She looked around Camilla's age or older.

"You must be Lindsey," the woman said.

"Yep, that's me," Lindsey replied. "Hi."

"My name is June. I'm the head housekeeper. Come with me."

Lindsey turned to grab her bags.

"Leave those. They'll be taken to your room."

Lindsey followed June into the manor. It was just as grand on the inside as it was outside. The entrance hall was vast and tall, with a huge chandelier hanging from the ceiling two stories up. Before them was a wide staircase that split into two at the top, branching off into each of the wings of the house.

"Let me take you to one of the guest suites," June said. "Camilla is still preparing your permanent rooms."

Rooms? As in, more than one? Lindsey followed June up the stairs and to the right, gaping at every room and hall they passed through. Everything was modern and new, but it had the elegance and sophistication of an old house. There were fireplaces and chandeliers everywhere. And Lindsey had thought Camilla was exaggerating when she said the house had over a hundred rooms, but it seemed like she was telling the truth.

June stopped in front of a door and opened it wide. "This is where you'll be staying for now."

Lindsey walked inside. It was like a five-star hotel room, complete with a massive bed and a spacious adjoining bathroom. And her suitcase and carry bag were right there in the room. How had they gotten there before her?

"If you ever need anything during your stay here, call

me. There's an intercom next to every door." June pointed to an intercom, which camouflaged surprisingly well with the house's decor. "I'll do my best to fulfill any requests personally. There are other staff who work here, but I'm the only one who is here 24/7, so you can seek me out at any time."

"Okay," Lindsey said.

"Now, would you like to relax and settle in? I can bring you refreshments? Or, I can give you a tour of the house."

Lindsey glanced at the plush bed. She was just dying to throw herself onto it. But she'd have time for that later. "A tour would be great."

June nodded. "Come with me."

Lindsey followed her out the door. June kept a brisk pace.

"Now, Camilla has said you're to have free run of the house while living here," June said. "That is, except for Camilla's rooms. I'll show you where they are when we get there."

They went back the direction they came. When they reached the entrance, June took Lindsey left and gestured down a hall.

"The east wing is that way," she said. "It's not in use anymore, and it hasn't been renovated like the rest of the house. All you'll find down there are empty rooms and peeling wallpaper."

They returned to the entrance hall and continued through the manor, from the ground floor up. June pointed out various rooms. There was a gym, a home theater, a library, even a lap pool. It was like there was a room for everything.

Finally, they reached a set of white double doors. June stopped before them. "These are Camilla's rooms. You're explicitly forbidden to go beyond this point. Camilla likes her privacy."

Lindsey nodded. "Where is Camilla, by the way?"

"Camilla will be with you when she can," June said.

What does that mean? But Lindsey could tell by June's expression that she shouldn't pry.

"Now, let me show you around outside. There are several gardens on the grounds as well as a swimming pool and tennis courts." June turned and started back down the hall. "There are stables too, but we haven't had horses here in years."

Lindsey glanced at the doors to Camilla's rooms one last time, then walked away.

It wasn't until later that evening that Lindsey finally got to test out her bed. It was just as comfy as it looked.

She sank into it and closed her eyes. This was the life. She'd spent the day exploring the manor and the grounds, taking in the beautiful scenery. The old Lindsey would have loved to sketch it. A small part of her wanted to. But she didn't have her art supplies anyway. She'd also found an overgrown hedge maze, which she'd quickly gotten lost in. When Lindsey had finally gotten out, she'd found a quiet corner in one of the gardens, among sculpted topiaries and marble statues, and called Faith to reassure her that Camilla hadn't kidnapped her.

Where was Camilla? June hadn't specified whether

Camilla was in the house or not. Lindsey found herself wishing Camilla had been the one to show her around the manor.

Her stomach rumbled. June had served Lindsey lunch after the tour. She hadn't eaten since then. She was debating whether to call June and ask, when there was a knock on her door.

Camilla? Lindsey leaped up and opened it. But instead of Camilla, she found June.

"Oh," Lindsey said. "Hi, June."

"Would you like to come down for dinner?" June asked. "Or, I can bring something up."

"I'll come down." Lindsey paused. "Is Camilla going to be there?"

"Not tonight."

"Why not? Is everything okay?"

"She's… indisposed," June said.

Lindsey frowned. What did she mean by that?

To Lindsey's surprise, June gave her a reserved, but sympathetic smile. "She'll be with you when she can. Now, let me take you to the dining room. Finding your way in this house can be difficult at first."

"Thanks, June," Lindsey said.

"No need to thank me. Camilla has instructed me to make you feel as at home as possible."

That was nice of her. But what Lindsey really wanted was to see Camilla.

Where was she?

CHAPTER SEVEN

The next morning, Camilla didn't appear at breakfast. By the afternoon, Lindsey still hadn't seen her, but she'd glimpsed June carrying a tray of food into Camilla's quarters after lunch.

Was this normal? Was this how it was going to be? It seemed unlikely that Camilla would pay Lindsey an outrageous amount of money to come live here if she wasn't going to spend any time with her.

Once again, Lindsey had spent most of the day exploring the grounds and the gardens. As she walked back inside, she almost ran into June.

The housekeeper was carrying a tray laden with tea, coffee, and pastries. "I was just coming to find you, Lindsey. Camilla wants to see you."

Finally. Lindsey had been starting to feel rejected.

"She's putting the finishing touches on your rooms. She wants you to meet her there. I'll take you to her."

"Thanks," Lindsey said.

She followed June upstairs and through the maze of a house. They came to an open door. June stopped before it.

"Your rooms are through there," June said. "She's waiting for you."

Lindsey paused at the doorway. She'd been waiting for this moment ever since she arrived, and her anticipation had only grown. She pulled herself together and entered the room.

It wasn't a bedroom like she expected. It looked like a kind of sitting room, with several doors coming off it. Camilla was seated on a lounge in the middle of the room. She looked as elegant and put-together as on their first date, although she was dressed more casually. She certainly didn't look like she'd been 'indisposed.'

"Lindsey." Camilla gestured to the seat across from her. "Come. Sit."

Lindsey sat down. June set the tray of refreshments on the coffee table and began to lay everything out.

"Sorry I wasn't able to come and greet you yesterday," Camilla said.

"It's okay," Lindsey replied. "Is everything all right? June said you were indisposed."

"Did she now?" Camilla gave June a sharp look. "I assure you, I'm fine. I have quite a lot to do, but I wanted to take a moment to show you your rooms and talk about our arrangement." She paused and waited for June to finish setting everything out.

June straightened up and wiped her hands on her apron. "Is there anything else you need?"

"No, that will be all," Camilla said. "Thank you."

With a nod, June disappeared.

Camilla waved a hand toward the table. "Help yourself."

"Thanks." Lindsey picked up a pastry.

"Now, I hate to start on such a serious note, but there's a lot that we need to discuss," Camilla said. "Firstly, house rules. June tells me she's already shown you around. You're free to go wherever you like, except for my rooms. They're off limits unless you're with me, understand?"

Lindsey nodded. Camilla's manner suddenly reminded her of a teacher she'd had in middle school, who could turn from warm and kind to serious and stern at the flick of a switch. And if you did something to disappoint her, she became as cold as ice.

Lindsey had always liked that teacher.

"Everything in the house is at your disposal," Camilla said. "If you need anything at all, ask June. My only request is that you treat her with respect. She's not a servant. She's kept this house running for the last 15 years. And it's far too hard to find good help these days."

"Okay," Lindsey said.

"You're also free to come and go as you like. If you want to go somewhere, ask June to call you a car. I'd prefer it if you let me know if you're leaving."

"I will."

"I ask that you avoid leaving the grounds when we have plans to spend time together." Camilla folded her hands in her lap. "Which brings me to our schedule. Breakfast is at 8 a.m. After breakfast, I'll retire to my study to work, and you'll be free to do whatever you want. Lunch is at midday. After lunch, I like to take an hour or so to relax, during which time you'll join me. In the afternoon, I'll return to my study until dinner. And after dinner, the evenings are for us to spend together."

"Okay." Lindsey was beginning to understand why Camilla's exes had called her a control freak.

"Now, about our arrangement," Camilla said. "If at any point you have a problem with any part of it, tell me. I don't want you to ever feel pressured or uncomfortable. Dominant/submissive relationships are complicated enough, even without our unusual circumstances. Communication is essential."

Lindsey nodded.

"Have you chosen your safeword?"

"Yes. Apple."

"Good," Camilla said. "Use it whenever you feel you need to. Even if you simply want a time out from our day-to-day routine. It's not like I'm going to be leading you around the house on a leash, but being a submissive 24/7 can be hard. If it gets exhausting, let me know."

Lindsey nodded. "I will."

"Otherwise, if you break any of my rules or the rules of this house, a punishment will be in order."

Punishments were one of Camilla's non-negotiable requirements, but she promised she'd never use them without a good reason. Lindsey didn't mind. And mercifully, Camilla had allowed Lindsey to choose her own from a very long list. Lindsey had picked the punishments which seemed the least severe. Cleaning, writing lines, time-outs. But she didn't expect that Camilla would go easy on her. It was clear that Camilla was a harsh Mistress. Yes, Camilla was going to spoil her. But she demanded a lot in return.

"I have this schedule and these rules for a reason. I don't like disruptions to my routine. And I don't like surprises."

Lindsey nodded.

"Do you have any objections?" Camilla asked. "Or, is there anything you'd like to negotiate?"

Lindsey shook her head, then remembered herself. "No, Mistress."

A hint of a smile crossed Camilla's lips. "Good. I'd love to stay and chat, but unfortunately, I have work to do. However, I want to make it up to you for being absent this past day or two. How would you like to have dinner in the courtyard garden tonight? I have a chef on call who makes the most delectable French cuisine."

"I would like that, Mistress."

"Good. Wear something nice. The emerald halter-neck dress is perfect for the occasion."

"What dress?" Lindsey asked.

"I bought you a few things. Have a look inside the closet in your bedroom once I'm gone." Camilla stood up. "I'll see you tonight."

As soon as Camilla left the room, Lindsey got up and located her bedroom. It was just like the guest room she'd been staying in, only larger, and it had its own balcony with a view of the grounds. After admiring the room, Lindsey walked over to the closet and opened the doors.

"Wow."

Inside was what had to be a whole new wardrobe. Formal dresses, casual wear, and everything in between. She even had workout clothes and swimwear, as well as shoes and all sorts of accessories.

This was more than 'a few things.' It was everything she could possibly need.

Lindsey grinned. She was going to like it here.

Later that evening, Lindsey went out into the courtyard garden to join Camilla for dinner. As instructed, she wore the emerald dress she'd found in her closet. She'd paired it with some silver earrings and a necklace she'd found in a jewelry box on her dressing table.

Camilla was already seated on an outdoor lounge nearby, a bottle of wine and two glasses on the table next to her. Like Lindsey, she was dressed in a cocktail dress, but hers was a vibrant blue. She spotted Lindsey and smiled. "That dress looks just as lovely on you as I imagined. It brings out that striking red hair of yours."

"Thank you, Mistress," Lindsey replied.

Camilla gestured to the seat next to her. "Sit."

Lindsey sat down and looked around. She'd spent some time in this garden yesterday during the daytime. It looked lovelier at night. At the other end of the courtyard, June was setting a table for the two of them.

Camilla picked up the bottle from the table beside her and held it up. "Wine?"

"Yes, please," Lindsey said.

Camilla poured two glasses of wine and handed one to Lindsey. "So, how are you finding the house so far?"

"I love it. It's so beautiful."

"It's been in my family for generations. I inherited it after my parents passed." Camilla turned her gaze toward the manor. "You should have seen it 25 years ago. It was so much livelier. We had horses in the stables, and the orchard was carefully tended. And my parents were always throwing parties. Of course, back then the house had a full-time staff. I downsized when I took over. That's why the east wing is closed. Keeping the entire house running is almost impossible."

"I can imagine," Lindsey said. "This place is so big. I've already gotten lost a few times."

"It can take some getting used to," Camilla said. "Let me know if there's anything you need. This is going to be your home for the next three months after all."

"Thank you, Mistress. You've done enough for me already."

"I take it you found your new things, then?" Camilla said. "It's all yours, by the way. You can take everything with you when you leave."

"Seriously?" Lindsey asked. "Thank you! Not that I'm complaining, but you didn't have to do all that."

"It's no trouble. And I did promise to spoil you. You'll have the best of everything while you're here. Besides, there's something immensely satisfying about lavishing an appreciative woman with gifts."

"I definitely appreciate it," Lindsey said. "Thank you, Mistress."

"You're very welcome," Camilla replied. "Now, we haven't had a chance to properly discuss your answers to that questionnaire. Who knew you had such wicked desires hidden away in that innocent head of yours?"

Lindsey's face began to burn. She wasn't at all shy about

her unusual appetites, but Camilla had a way of getting under her skin.

"I have a question for you," Camilla said. "Of all the kinky things you like, what is it that you like the most?"

"Well," Lindsey thought for a moment. "I like being spanked. It's not that I like that it hurts. I just like the way it makes me feel."

"And me bringing up how naughty you are makes you feel the same way, doesn't it?" Camilla lowered her voice. "It hasn't escaped my notice that every time I do, you turn a delicious shade of red."

Lindsey's face grew even hotter, making Camilla chuckle.

"What about you, Mistress?" Lindsey asked. "What do you like the most?"

"Personally, bondage is my tool of choice," Camilla said. "Handcuffs, ropes, even suspension. There's something so intoxicating about having a sweet, willing submissive all bound up for me. And based on your answers to the questionnaire, you would enjoy that too."

"Yes, Mistress." Just thinking about it gave Lindsey a rush.

"But blindfolds are a soft limit for you, correct?"

Lindsey nodded. She had quite a few hard limits, most of which were activities that most people would consider extreme, but blindfolds were her only limit that was negotiable. "I don't know why I'm fine with bondage, but not blindfolds. I guess if someone is going to tie me up and flog me I want to see it coming."

Camilla laughed. "That's fair."

"But it's a soft limit for a reason. I do want to try it

sometime. I'd just have to be really comfortable with someone to do it."

"I understand. It requires a lot of trust. So, no blindfolds. Or anything else that you haven't explicitly agreed to."

Sex. Camilla had made it clear that she wasn't going to cross that line without the go-ahead from Lindsey. But Lindsey was starting to wonder if she should just give in to her curiosity.

"That still leaves us with a lot of options," Camilla said. "I have a very well stocked playroom."

"Seriously?" Lindsey said. "You have a playroom in your house?"

"Darling, the manor has its own ballroom. The first thing I did when I inherited this place was to convert one of the rooms into a playroom."

"Can I see it?"

"That depends," Camilla said. "I don't let anyone into my playroom who isn't prepared to play."

"I am," Lindsey said. "I want to. Please, Mistress?"

Camilla's hazel eyes searched Lindsey's face.

"All right," she said. "We'll have dessert in the playroom. Would you like that?"

Lindsey smiled. "I would, Mistress."

"Then it's settled." Camilla got up and offered her hand to Lindsey. "But first, dinner."

CHAPTER EIGHT

Lindsey followed Camilla down the winding halls of the manor and through the white doors that separated Camilla's rooms from the rest of the house. It was the first time she'd been in this forbidden part of the mansion. It was large enough to make up a house all by itself.

Camilla led Lindsey to a nondescript door and opened it wide. The two of them entered the room. It looked like nothing more than another of the manor's luxurious bedrooms. Unlike the rest of the house, the room was all dark tones, mostly purples and blues, but the lushness of the decor made it feel cozy and warm. There was a huge four-poster bed in the middle, complete with a canopy and curtains made from dark voile. The sheer drapes were tied to the bedposts with velvet ties.

"This is the playroom?" Lindsey asked.

"What were you expecting?" Camilla said. "Some kind of dungeon with chains and shackles?"

"Well, yeah. And where are all the toys?"

"I like to keep everything hidden away so that there are no distractions. I prefer my submissive to be relaxed and focused on me."

Lindsey looked around. There was more storage in the room than a usual bedroom. Cupboards, closets, chests. What secret treasures did they contain?

There was a knock on the playroom door.

"That must be June with dessert." Camilla gestured toward a small table at the side of the room. "Have a seat. I'll be right back."

Lindsey walked over to the table and sat down. Camilla slipped out into the hall, shutting the door behind her. Moments later, she returned, balancing a tray covered with a silver lid in her hands. She placed it in the center of the table.

Lindsey watched her eagerly. It was clear that Camilla planned for them to do more than just eat dessert. Sure enough, Camilla walked over to a cabinet and opened the door. Inside were a variety of restraints. Ropes, leather cuffs lined with fur, heavy-duty handcuffs, belts. Lindsey was sure she spotted a spreader bar too.

Camilla picked up a coil of thick black rope. She ran it through her hands from end to end, straightening out the kinks, and brought the rope over to Lindsey. "Cross your wrists at the back of the chair."

Lindsey obeyed. Camilla crouched behind her and wound the rope around Lindsey's wrists, tying them with a series of knots. When she was done, Lindsey tested her bonds. They were unyielding.

Camilla sat down across from Lindsey and removed the cover from the tray. What was underneath almost made

Lindsey drool. It was a spread of sweet treats. Fruit, chocolate fondue, and all kinds of tiny confections.

"Doesn't this look marvelous?" Camilla said.

"Yes, Mistress." Lindsey wanted to try everything.

Then she remembered her hands were tied behind her back.

Camilla picked up a plump blood-red grape and dipped it in chocolate. She slipped it between her lips and closed her eyes, chewing slowly.

"Mm, this tastes wonderful." Camilla selected a bright red strawberry, the same color as her lips, and slid it into her mouth. "This is my one weakness. I love all things sweet." She reached across the table and drew a finger down Lindsey's cheek, leaving behind a streak of chocolate.

Suddenly, Lindsey found herself with a craving that had little to do with dessert.

Camilla took another strawberry and dipped it into the chocolate. She held it up before Lindsey. "Would you like to try one?"

"Yes please," Lindsey said.

Camilla slipped the strawberry into Lindsey's waiting mouth.

Lindsey let out an involuntary moan. "This is incredible."

"The strawberries were picked fresh this morning. The chocolate is made from the finest Ghanaian cocoa beans. Here." Camilla picked up a small square of dark chocolate. "Try some by itself."

Lindsey leaned forward, accepting Camilla's offering. It was bitter and rich in Lindsey's mouth. Camilla went through the tray, sampling everything before feeding a portion to Lindsey. There was something alluring about watching her Mistress eat. Was it the way her lips would purse around each tiny morsel? The blissful sounds she made? The tantalizing looks she gave Lindsey every time she picked out a sweet treat?

Lindsey had never thought that having things fed to her could be so sensual. Now and then, Camilla's fingers would brush against Lindsey's lips, sending a frisson through her.

"That's enough for now," Camilla said. "I don't want you stuffed full for what comes next."

"What comes next?" Lindsey asked.

"Next, I'm going to give you a sampler of all my favorite spanking toys. Would you like that?"

Lindsey's breath quickened. "Yes, Mistress."

Camilla went over to a cabinet, a different one this time, and pulled out a long, black leather roll with a velvet tie around it. Lindsey was reminded of a roll-up case she used to carry her paintbrushes around. But this one was longer than Camilla's arm.

"Go lie on the bed on your stomach," Camilla said.

Lindsey got up from the chair, which was a feat in itself with her hands tied behind her back. As she climbed onto the four-poster bed, she noticed that peeking out from the curtains at the foot of the bed was an X built into the frame, made up from the same dark wood. Camilla said she liked to tie up submissives. Would Camilla one day tie Lindsey to it?

Lindsey lay down on her stomach, her head tilted to one side to watch Camilla. Camilla untied the roll, set it down, and unraveled it along the bed next to Lindsey. The roll had a dozen long, thin pockets. But instead of paint brushes, it contained a variety of whips, crops, and canes. There were also a handful of short paddles and floggers as well as a few implements Lindsey had never seen before.

"First, I'm going to get you all warmed up," Camilla said.

She dragged her fingers up the back of Lindsey's legs, all the way to the top of her thighs. Her hands stayed above Lindsey's dress. Camilla was staying true to her word not to cross any boundaries. But right now, Lindsey was ready to throw those boundaries out the window.

"Move your hands," Camilla said.

Lindsey lifted her bound wrists up to the middle of her back.

Camilla raised a hand and slapped Lindsey on her ass cheeks, over and over. Lindsey cried out, her skin sparking with electricity. It barely hurt. But with every slap came the perverse thrill of being punished, of enjoying something that she knew she shouldn't, the taboo of playing at a game so deliciously twisted. All those feelings blended together made a heady cocktail.

After a minute or so, Camilla stopped. She straightened up and surveyed the roll of spanking tools before her. "Let's go from the mildest to the most intense. I'll start with this."

Camilla grabbed one of the paddles from the roll. It was large, flat, and made of hard leather. She flexed it a few times in her hands.

"Didn't I tell you to lie on your stomach?" Camilla said.

"Sorry, Mistress." Lindsey hadn't even realized she'd rolled onto her side to watch Camilla.

"I know this excites you, but I expect you to follow my instructions."

Camilla spanked Lindsey with the paddle a few times,

ramping up the force. Each hit made a loud slap that made Lindsey jump and squirm.

"That's all?" Camilla said. "I was expecting much more of a reaction. I'll have to try something with a little more bite." She tossed the paddle to the side, then pulled out a short whip with dozens of tails. "Like this flogger."

She flicked the flogger across Lindsey's ass cheeks. It hit with a heavy sting that made Lindsey yelp.

Camilla whipped her a few more times. "Better. But I don't think we're there yet." Camilla reached into the roll again. "Let's try a quirt."

The item she produced was a short whip, this time with only two thick tails. Lindsey had never seen one like it before. Camilla struck Lindsey with it. She sucked in a breath, the sharp kiss of the tails penetrating deep. Lindsey wriggled and pulled at the ropes around her wrists as Camilla brought the quirt down over and over.

Camilla stroked her hand down Lindsey's arm. "Still okay there?"

"Yes, Mistress." Lindsey craved more. Of Camilla's touch, of the whip, of everything.

"Just one more." Tossing the quirt aside, Camilla picked out a long thin riding crop and flexed it in her hands. "Actually, I think what you really need is a firmer hand."

Camilla returned the riding crop to its place and reached into the pocket next to it, selecting a thick rattan cane. She swung it through the air a few times. It made a sharp, cutting swoosh.

"The cane can be intense, but I think it's exactly what you need. Some old-school discipline for a very wicked sub."

Camilla's words made Lindsey's whole body pulse. She shut her eyes, waiting for that telltale swoosh.

But it all happened at the same time. Lindsey heard the sound and felt the sting on her cheeks simultaneously. Lindsey gasped. Camilla struck her again, once, twice, three times. Every blow vibrated through her, traveling up her spine, down to her toes, and right between her legs.

Camilla slid her hand down to caress Lindsey's ass cheeks over her dress. "You like that, don't you?"

"Yes, Mistress," Lindsey said.

Camilla swatted her with the cane again, over and over. She writhed on the bed, helpless with her arms restrained, adrenaline and arousal rushing through her veins.

She felt Camilla's hand on the back of her shoulder. "That's enough for tonight."

Lindsey whimpered. Her body was awake now. She didn't want things to be over yet.

"Don't worry, we have three whole months to explore all this. I'm going to untie you now."

Camilla unbound the ropes from Lindsey's wrists, releasing her. Lindsey rolled onto her back and flexed her hands, letting out a contented sigh.

Camilla placed the rope to the side, then slipped onto the bed beside Lindsey. "Did you enjoy that?"

Lindsey nodded. "Thank you, Mistress."

Camilla pecked Lindsey on the lips. "There's water on the nightstand next to you. And we still have all that dessert if you're hungry."

"I'm okay." There was something Lindsey wanted, but it wasn't food.

"Then there's only one thing left to do."

Camilla untied the sheer drapes, letting them fall around the bed. Like magic, the outside world disappeared, and it was just the two of them. Camilla wrapped her arms around Lindsey and drew her in close.

Lindsey purred. She liked the feel of Camilla's body against hers, in more ways than one. She knew Camilla's intentions weren't sexual. All of this was just standard aftercare. Camilla was looking after her submissive's needs, making sure Lindsey was warm, fed, hydrated, and most of all, offered comfort and affection to prevent her from crashing both physically and mentally.

But Lindsey didn't want comfort. She didn't want food or water or anything else.

She wanted Camilla.

Camilla kissed her again. This time, Lindsey kissed her back with double the intensity. Lindsey felt a shift in her Mistress's body, a response to Lindsey's obvious hunger. She parted her lips and let Camilla's tongue dance around hers, desire flaring inside her.

Camilla pulled away. Lindsey whimpered in protest.

"What is it?" Camilla asked.

Lindsey's words caught in her throat. She was feeling so many things that she wasn't expecting to feel, and she found it impossible to articulate them all. Instead, she reached out and pulled Camilla back to her.

"Is there something you want?" Camilla's teasing tone made it clear that she already knew the answer.

Lindsey finally found her voice. "You know what I want, Mistress."

"We haven't discussed this part of our arrangement yet."

Lindsey groaned. "Please?"

"I did tell you that I take consent very seriously. I wouldn't want to cross any boundaries." Camilla traced her thumb down Lindsey's chin. "I'll make an exception, just this once. But you're going to have to tell me exactly what you want."

Lindsey nodded. Her chin tingled where Camilla had touched her.

"Tell me," Camilla said softly. "What do you want your Mistress to do for you?"

"Mistress, please." Lindsey's voice quivered. "Take off my dress."

Camilla reached around behind Lindsey and unzipped the emerald-green dress, her hands brushing down Lindsey's naked back. A shiver spread over her skin. Lindsey sat up, allowing Camilla to pull it off. She wasn't wearing a bra underneath the low-backed dress, and her nipples perked up in the cool air. Lindsey lay back down on her side facing Camilla.

"What else?" Camilla asked. "What else do you want me to do?"

"Mistress, please," Lindsey said. "Touch me."

"Like this?" Camilla drew her hand down the front of Lindsey's body, snaking her fingertips down her shoulders and over her chest.

"Yes, Mistress. Like that."

Camilla's hands wandered all over Lindsey's bare skin gently, as if she were touching something precious. Lindsey murmured with bliss.

"Mistress, please," Lindsey said. "May I touch you?"

"Yes," Camilla replied.

Lindsey reached out and swept her fingers along Camilla's side, from her knee, up her thigh, and over her hip. She let her hand creep up the front of Camilla's chest. Her curves were so smooth and supple. Lindsey wanted to ask if she could take off Camilla's clothes, but the way Camilla's hands were exploring Lindsey's own body left her too distracted to focus on anything but her own pleasure.

"Mistress," Lindsey whispered. "Please kiss me."

"Where do you want me to kiss you?" Camilla asked.

"Everywhere."

Camilla pushed Lindsey's shoulder down to the bed so that she was lying on her back, then dipped low, kissing Lindsey's lips, and up behind her ear, and down the side of her throat. The touch of Camilla's soft lips made Lindsey's skin sprout goosebumps. Camilla painted a swathe of kisses down to Lindsey's breasts, then took a nipple in her mouth, circling it with her tongue.

"Oh god." Lindsey's head fell back, her toes curling to grip the sheet beneath her.

Camilla switched to the other nipple, her hands trailing down Lindsey's sides. Lindsey's chest rose up to meet her. Camilla's hands roamed down Lindsey's hips and thighs as she kissed Lindsey all the way down to her bellybutton.

"Mistress," Lindsey begged. But what did she want? She wanted Camilla to kiss her, to touch her, to fuck her, all at once. "Please-"

"Hush." Camilla looked up at her. "I haven't finished kissing you everywhere yet." Without breaking her gaze, Camilla took the waistband of Lindsey's panties and tugged them down her legs, then she pushed Lindsey's knees apart.

Lindsey trembled. Camilla grazed her lips along the curve of Lindsey's hipbone, down and inward to the apex of

Lindsey's thighs. Camilla kissed her way down Lindsey's slit, her mouth skimming over Lindsey's swollen bud.

"Oh!" A dart of pleasure went straight through to Lindsey's core.

Camilla ran her tongue up and down, gliding it over Lindsey's folds. Lindsey moaned. She had never been this wet in her life.

Finally, Camilla settled her lips at Lindsey's clit.

Lindsey seized hold of the pillow above her head, writhing against the sheets. Camilla licked and sucked, harder now, every movement of her tongue bringing Lindsey closer to oblivion. Lindsey's eyes rolled into the back of her head, the pressure inside her mounting.

"Mistress!" Lindsey convulsed on the bed as an orgasm rippled through her. She clutched at the sheets, holding on as if to keep herself from getting washed away. Camilla didn't stop until Lindsey sank back down to the bed, whispering the word Mistress like it was a prayer.

Camilla slid back up beside her and pressed her lips to Lindsey's. Lindsey melted into the kiss.

"Mistress," she said. "Thank you."

Camilla settled next to her. Lindsey rested her head in the crook of her Mistress's neck.

But as her haze of bliss cleared, it was replaced by confusion. She'd just had the most mind-blowing sex of her life. With Camilla. A woman.

Maybe she wasn't as straight as she thought she was.

CHAPTER NINE

Lindsey made her way down to the dining room for breakfast. Over a week had passed since she'd arrived, and she had finally learned how to get around the house. And she and Camilla were beginning to get into a routine. Camilla followed her schedule to the letter and spent most of the day working. But they always had meals together and spent long, lazy evenings lounging around before retiring to their separate bedrooms.

Since that night in the playroom, they hadn't returned there, and they hadn't had sex again either. They'd had a long discussion about it. Considering the nature of their relationship, Camilla wanted to make sure that Lindsey was comfortable and didn't feel pressured in any way. Lindsey appreciated Camilla's respect for her boundaries. But she didn't feel pressured. If anything, it was the opposite. She just wanted more.

Camilla had awakened something in Lindsey that night. Her attraction toward Camilla had gone from a vague sense of admiration to something much more real, and Lindsey didn't know what to make of it. Was it just Camilla's dominant side that had the submissive in Lindsey so deeply enthralled? It wasn't real attraction, was it?

When Lindsey reached the dining room, Camilla was already seated at the head of the table, reading a newspaper while she waited for Lindsey. Even though it was 8 a.m., she looked flawlessly put-together, as usual. Perfect hair, light makeup, a stylish blouse and skirt that had to be designer. Despite the fact that she wasn't leaving the manor today, Camilla looked like she was ready to take on the world. Lindsey suspected that Camilla dressed like this every day, even when she was alone in the house.

Lindsey walked over to the table. Several dishes were laid out, and a place was set for Lindsey next to Camilla. June placed a vase of freshly cut flowers in the middle of the table.

"Good morning, Lindsey." Camilla tilted her head for Lindsey to plant a kiss on her cheek.

"Good morning, Mistre-" Lindsey clamped her mouth shut. June was standing right there. Lindsey had never called Camilla "Mistress" in front of anyone else.

"Oh, don't worry about June," Camilla said. "She sees and hears nothing. Isn't that right, June?"

"I'm sorry Ma'am," June said. "I didn't catch that."

"You see? Have a seat, Lindsey."

Lindsey sat down. As June left the room, Lindsey was certain she saw the slightest smirk on the housekeeper's face.

She and Camilla helped themselves to breakfast. It seemed like the spread laid out before them was for Lindsey's benefit. Camilla always ate the same thing—poached eggs on toast with a side of grilled mushrooms and a cup of coffee. Camilla was serious about her coffee. It was one of her many indulgences.

"What do you have planned for the day, Mistress?" Lindsey asked.

"The usual. Work, work, and more work. I'm up to my elbows in paperwork. And I have a video conference with the heads of one of our subsidiaries. There have been some irregularities-" Camilla stopped short. "I'm boring you."

"No, you're not. I like hearing about your job." Lindsey was beginning to enjoy their conversations about even the most mundane things.

"What about you?" Camilla asked. "What's on for the day?"

"I brought a few books with me, so I'm going to start reading them. I never had the time to read when I was working full-time at the call center. And I might go for a swim in the pool later."

"That sounds lovely." Camilla frowned. "Where's June with the coffee?"

As the two of them ate, Lindsey examined Camilla's face. She seemed a little stressed. Lindsey wondered if she should say something, but she wasn't sure if it would help.

After a while, Camilla spoke. "Tonight, after dinner. Why don't we watch a movie together? The theater is very well equipped."

Lindsey swallowed her mouthful of food. "I would like that, Mistress."

Camilla seemed to perk up a bit at that. But it wasn't to

last. A moment later, June returned to the dining room with a pot of coffee.

"I'm sorry, Ma'am," she said. "We've run out of the Brazilian coffee beans you like."

"Really, June?" Camilla said. "Again?"

"The suppliers have run out. I found you a Colombian blend that's very similar. Just until we can get more."

"That will have to do." Camilla waved June over.

June poured Camilla a cup of coffee and scurried out of the room. Camilla didn't even give her as much as a thank you. She knew Camilla hated any deviations from her routine, but this seemed like an overreaction.

Camilla pushed away her plate, which she'd barely touched, and stood up. "I'm going to get to work. I'll see you at lunchtime." Without another word, Camilla picked up her cup of coffee and left the dining room.

Midday arrived, but Camilla didn't come down for lunch. Lindsey assumed it was because she was busy with work. But when dinnertime rolled around, and Camilla didn't emerge from her rooms, Lindsey began to wonder whether something was wrong. It was just like the first few days after Lindsey had arrived.

As Lindsey finished off her dinner, June entered the dining room. "Is there anything else you need?"

"I'm good," Lindsey said. "Is everything okay with Camilla?"

"Everything is fine."

"Then why didn't she come down for dinner?"

"Look," June said. "You should probably get used to this. It happens with Camilla sometimes."

"But why?" Lindsey asked. "What's going on?"

"It's not my place to say. And I'd recommend that you don't ask her about it either. Let her tell you if and when she wants to."

"Is she okay, at least?"

"Yes, she's all right. Is there anything else I can do for you?"

Lindsey took the hint. "No. Thanks, June."

June nodded and began clearing the table. Lindsey got up and headed back to her room. It was safe to say that her and Camilla's plan to watch a movie together was canceled.

Lindsey sighed. Things had gone from wonderful to confusing in the space of a few days. She thought about calling Faith to talk. Although they had spoken yesterday, Lindsey hadn't told Faith that she'd had sex with Camilla. She didn't think Faith would understand why Lindsey felt so uneasy about it. Faith's Zen attitude to life never helped when Lindsey was worried about something. And these days, all she did was worry.

Lindsey stopped at the bottom of the stairs. She would have to find some way to entertain herself for the rest of the night. She decided to check out the home theater by herself. A movie night was just what she needed.

All she had to do was find the theater. Lindsey knew it was on the second floor somewhere. She could ask June, but Lindsey didn't like bothering her over small things. She still wasn't used to having 'help,' which was what Camilla called the mostly invisible staff who ran the house.

Lindsey headed upstairs and began to wander, opening

doors at random. She found the library, and the gym, but no theater. She was sure it was nearby, but everything looked different at night.

Lindsey continued down the hall. Soon, she found herself facing a set of white double doors.

The doors to Camilla's rooms.

Lindsey stopped before them. Camilla had made it clear that Lindsey wasn't allowed past this point without her express permission. But Lindsey was tired of being kept in the dark. And she was worried. Camilla had seemed off at breakfast in the morning. What if something was wrong?

Tentatively, Lindsey pulled one of the doors open and peeked past them into the hall. It was empty. She glanced over her shoulder. No one else was around. She slipped through the door and closed it behind her.

Lindsey started down the hall. What was she doing in here, anyway? Was she going to knock on Camilla's door and try to talk to her? Spy on her just to make sure she was in one piece? Burst in and demand to know what was going on?

Lindsey rounded a corner. When she reached the door to the playroom, she paused in front of it. All kinds of naughty thoughts about the other night filled her mind. As she stood there silently, she heard voices coming from the end of the hall.

Raised voices.

Before Lindsey knew what she was doing, she was walking toward the voices. As she got closer, they became clearer.

"I pay you to look after the house, not to nag me."

Camilla. Her voice was shrill. "I should replace you with someone who actually follows my orders."

What the hell? Lindsey stopped at the door to the room the voices were coming from. It was open, just a crack, but Lindsey couldn't see through it. She listened instead.

"We both know you're not going to do that, Camilla." *June?* It was June's voice, but it had a firmer, less deferential tone. And Lindsey had never heard June address Camilla by anything other than 'Ma'am.'

"Will you just leave me alone?" Camilla said.

"Sure, I'll leave you alone. Right after you eat something."

"Do I look like I want to eat anything?"

"There's no better time than now," June said. "Those painkillers should have kicked in."

"Well, they aren't doing shit."

"I'm sorry, Camilla. But you still need to eat. You haven't eaten anything all day."

Camilla let out a groan that made Lindsey's stomach lurch.

Against her better judgment, Lindsey pushed the door open even more, just enough so that she could see inside. The large room was dark, lit by a single lamp next to Camilla's bed at the far side of the room. Lindsey could only just make out Camilla's figure on the bed, curled up in a ball, the sheets twisted around her. Her hair clung to her forehead, and her cheeks were pale.

"Come on, Camilla." June was seated in an armchair by the bed, her arms crossed. A covered silver serving tray sat on the nightstand next to her. "You've been running yourself into the ground lately. You can't afford to not look after yourself. You know that just makes things worse."

Camilla uttered a curse which Lindsey was shocked to hear come out of her mouth. "Fine. If it'll get you off my case."

"Good." June picked up the tray from the nightstand. "And will you be getting out of bed, Ma'am?"

"I'll sit at the table," Camilla said through gritted teeth. "I hope you're happy."

"In a few days, you'll be happy that you got out of bed. The last thing either of us needs is you stomping around the house, angry that you let yourself lie around doing nothing."

"I hate that you're right," Camilla grumbled.

"I'd be pretty bad at my job if I hadn't figured out what you're like after all these years." June got up and turned toward the table at the other side of the room.

The table that was right between the bed and the door.

Shit. Before Lindsey could act, June spotted her and froze.

Camilla turned toward where June was looking. "What-" Her eyes locked onto Lindsey's, and her face clouded over.

Lindsey's every instinct told her to shut the door and get out of there as quickly as possible. But Camilla's eyes held her there. And even from this distance, Lindsey could see every emotion boiling within them. Surprise. Disappointment. Anger. Betrayal.

Lindsey's heart sank. She had messed up. She had seen something Camilla didn't want her to see. But Lindsey's concern outweighed her guilt. Camilla could yell and scream at her all she wanted. She just needed to know that Camilla was okay.

But Lindsey didn't get the chance to ask. Her eyes still on Lindsey's, Camilla spoke, her cold voice cutting through the air.

"Close the door, June."

"Yes, Ma'am." The housekeeper walked over to the door and shut it in Lindsey's face.

CHAPTER TEN

"Why won't you tell me what's going on?" Lindsey asked.

June began clearing dinner from the table, stacking the dishes on the dining cart next to her. "We've been through this. All you need to know is that she's okay."

It had been two days since Lindsey had witnessed the scene in Camilla's room. Two days, and she still hadn't seen Camilla. Lindsey had asked June about her a dozen times, but the housekeeper remained tight-lipped. Even more infuriatingly, June continued to act like nothing had happened at all.

"She didn't look okay." Lindsey's mind went back to that night. She'd gone over it again and again in her head. From what Lindsey had overheard, it sounded like it was something that happened a lot. Was Camilla sick? Was there something seriously wrong with her? Was she dying? Naturally, her mind went to the worst possible explanations. "If she's okay, why is she still locked up in her rooms?"

"She's not locked up," June said. "She has everything she needs."

"Can't you just tell me what's wrong with her?" Lindsey's voice shook. "Please, June."

June stopped what she was doing. "Look, it's not my place to say. Camilla doesn't like to talk about it."

"Camilla can speak for herself."

Lindsey and June turned to the doorway where Camilla stood. She was dressed in a pale pink satin robe, her brown hair hanging loose. She looked a lot better than the other night, but she seemed drained, and her lips were pressed in a thin line.

"Good evening, Ma'am," June said, as if nothing was out of the ordinary. "Would you like some dinner?"

"Later," Camilla replied. "I need to have a word with Lindsey."

Oh. Lindsey had been so worried about Camilla that she hadn't given much thought to the fact that she'd gone into Camilla's rooms when Camilla had expressly forbidden it.

And Camilla looked furious.

"I'll get out of your hair." June grabbed the cart of dishes and practically sprinted out of the room.

Camilla strode to the head of the table and sat down. "Lindsey." She clasped her hands in front of her. "We need to talk about the other night."

Lindsey's stomach stirred. Camilla's face was hard and cold. Just how mad was she? Would she throw Lindsey out? End their arrangement? Lindsey didn't care at that point. She just wanted to know that Camilla was all right.

"I'm sorry you had to see me like that," Camilla said.

"What do you mean?" Lindsey asked. "I just want to know what's going on. Are you okay?"

"I'm fine. I have a chronic medical condition called endometriosis."

"What's that?"

"It's what happens when the tissue that lines the uterus starts growing in other places in the body," Camilla said. "Places where it shouldn't grow."

Lindsey frowned. That sounded horrifying.

"It's relatively benign. But it causes some problems with inflammation and pain, as well as a laundry list of other symptoms. If you want the grisly details, you can look it up."

"Is it going to kill you?" Lindsey asked.

"What? No, not at all." Camilla paused. "You were that worried?"

"Of course I was! You just disappeared without a word, for the second time, and then I saw you curled up in bed in too much pain to eat, talking about taking painkillers and yelling at June to leave you alone! What was I supposed to think?"

Camilla's expression softened. "You're right. I'm sorry. I would have spoken to you sooner if I knew you were so concerned. I assure you, I have a long and full life ahead of me, okay?"

Lindsey nodded.

"Now, is there anything else?"

"No." Lindsey had a million other questions, but it was clear that Camilla didn't want to discuss this any further.

"That's not all I wanted to speak to you about," Camilla said. "You came into my rooms without my permission. You invaded my privacy. You broke one of my rules."

"I'm sorry." Lindsey looked down at the table. "I was just worried about you."

"That doesn't change the fact that my rooms are off limits. You agreed to the rules when you came here. And you agreed that if you broke them, you would be punished."

Crap. Lindsey had forgotten all about that part of their agreement.

"I want five hundred lines. 'I will not go into my Mistress's rooms without her permission.' Five hundred lines, neat and legible."

"Yes, Mistress," Lindsey replied.

"I'll check on your progress tomorrow night." With that, Camilla got up and marched out of the room.

Lindsey put down her pen and flexed her fingers. She'd spent most of the day at the desk in her sitting room, writing "I will not go into my Mistress's rooms without her permission" over and over again, and she had barely made any progress.

She let out a groan of frustration. At this rate, it would take her days! Lindsey had chosen writing lines as a punishment because she thought it would be easier than the other options, but she hadn't anticipated the number of lines Camilla would make her write.

And real punishment was nowhere near as fun as the 'discipline' Camilla had doled out in the playroom that night.

Lindsey began again. *I will not go into my Mistress's rooms...*

She sighed. After she learned that Camilla was not, in fact, dying, she began to feel the weight of what she'd done. Lindsey hadn't just disobeyed Camilla's orders. She'd violated Camilla's privacy in a big way, and she'd seen Camilla at her most vulnerable. It was obvious that Camilla didn't like being vulnerable.

There was a knock on the door to Lindsey's sitting room. Was it Camilla, come to check on her? She got up and opened the door.

"Oh. I mean, hi June."

"I brought you some dinner." June held up a tray. "You didn't come down, so I thought you might be hungry."

"Thanks." Lindsey had been so busy writing lines that she'd lost track of time. Besides, her overwhelming guilt had caused her to lose her appetite.

"I'll set it up for you over there." June headed to the table by the window and set the tray down. She removed the lid and laid everything out. "Do you need anything else?"

"No." Lindsey paused. "Did Camilla go down for dinner?"

"No. She's still not feeling well."

"Oh."

"Are you all right?" June asked.

"I'm fine." But Lindsey couldn't keep her voice from quavering. "Thanks for bringing dinner."

June hovered by the table. "Lindsey, Camilla isn't angry with you."

"She seemed pretty angry to me," Lindsey said.

"Well, yes, she's angry with you. But she's mostly angry that she didn't get to choose how you found out about her illness."

"Did she say that?" Lindsey asked.

"No," June replied. "But I've known her for so long that it isn't hard for me to tell what's going on in her head." She patted Lindsey on the shoulder. "I'll come back for everything in an hour."

As June left the room, Lindsey noted to herself that for a woman who 'sees and hears nothing,' June sure knew a lot about what was going on between Lindsey and Camilla. But Lindsey was grateful. She was beginning to think she'd need an instruction manual to understand Camilla. And after the scene she'd witnessed, it was clear that June and Camilla were closer than they seemed.

As Lindsey ate her dinner, she thought on June's words. Maybe this punishment wasn't just because Lindsey had broken Camilla's rules. But it wasn't because she was mad at Lindsey either. Maybe it was Camilla's way of taking back control the way Lindsey had taken control away from Camilla.

A short while later, June returned to collect Lindsey's tray. When she was done clearing the table, June announced that Camilla wanted to see her.

"She's in her bedroom," June said. "Do you remember the way, or do you want me to take you?"

"I remember." Lindsey hesitated. "She said I should go to her room?"

June's lips curled up at one side. "I see you've learned your lesson. Yes, Camilla gave you her express permission to go to her room. She also said to 'bring your lines.' I'm assuming that means something to you."

Lindsey nodded. So there were things that June didn't

know about her and Camilla's relationship after all. Lindsey liked that she and Camilla still had their secrets.

"I recommend you don't keep her waiting," June said.

"Right. Thanks."

Once June had left the room, Lindsey grabbed her notepad and made her way to Camilla's wing. She was nowhere near finished with her lines yet, but at least she could show Camilla her progress.

Lindsey went through the white double doors and continued past the playroom until she reached Camilla's bedroom. She knocked on the door and waited.

"Come in," Camilla said.

Lindsey opened the door. The room looked a lot brighter than last time she'd seen it. Camilla was sitting up in bed, her legs stretched out and crossed at the ankles. She had a book face down on her lap. Although she didn't seem to be back to her normal self, she looked a lot better than the night before. But she still wore that same cold expression.

Camilla pointed to the bed next to her. "Come. Sit."

Lindsey sat down. "I'm sorry. I haven't finished my lines yet."

"It's all right." Camilla took the notepad from Lindsey's hand and placed it on the other side of the bed. "This isn't about the lines. I wanted to talk to you about everything that's happened."

"I'm sorry," Lindsey said again. "I know I shouldn't have gone into your rooms without permission, and I know I shouldn't have spied on you." Her lip quivered. "I'm sorry for forcing you to tell me about something you didn't want me to know about."

"Lindsey, it wasn't that I didn't want to tell you. What I wanted was to tell you on my terms. You found out in the worst way. And you saw me on one of my worst days in a long time. I wasn't ready to tell you. Not yet."

"You could have told me," Lindsey said. "I would have understood."

"It's always hard to know how someone will react. Most people react badly."

"How do you mean?"

"Where do I begin?" Camilla said. "There are the people who dismiss what I go through as 'lady problems,' or don't understand how debilitating it can be. They see me walking around and living life like everyone else, so they don't believe there is anything really wrong, and they think I'm just being lazy when I can't do things because I'm ill. It's the curse of an invisible illness."

"I would never think anything like that," Lindsey said.

"I wasn't afraid you would. Although it's frustrating, I can deal with people like that. What's worse is when people pity me." Camilla's eyes focused on something in the distance. "I don't want pity. I don't want to be told that it's amazing that I'm still able to live my life despite everything. Sure, it's hard sometimes. But that's just how it is for me. We all have to play the hand we've been dealt." Camilla gave Lindsey a half smile. "And I have to say, apart from my illness, I've been dealt a very good one."

Camilla's voice grew fainter. "I don't want you to treat me any differently. I don't want anything to change between us. And most of all, I don't want this to change the way you see me."

"Camilla." Lindsey placed her hand on Camilla's arm.

"This isn't going to change the way I see you. There's nothing that could make me see you as anything other than the strong, funny, beautiful woman you are. And I promise you. Nothing is going to change between us."

Camilla leaned over and kissed Lindsey on the forehead. "Consider your punishment over."

"Really? But I'm nowhere near finished."

"I'm feeling generous. No more lines. But there's something else I need you to do."

"Anything, Mistress," Lindsey said.

Camilla patted the spot on the bed next to her. "Stay here and keep me company for a while."

Lindsey climbed onto the enormous bed and sat down next to Camilla. After a moment or so, she placed her head in Camilla's lap. Camilla's hand fell to Lindsey's head. She stroked her fingers through Lindsey's hair.

A feeling of warmth spread through her. She still had plenty of questions she wanted to ask Camilla, but they could wait for another time.

Camilla broke the silence. "Tell me something about yourself. Something I don't know."

"Uh," Lindsey racked her brains. "I have the same birthday as Benjamin Franklin?"

"That's interesting, but not what I meant. Something meaningful."

Lindsey was silent for a moment. "I used to want to be an artist. I went to art school and everything. But I gave up on the idea after I graduated."

"Oh?" Camilla said. "What changed?"

Lindsey shrugged. "I grew up."

Camilla brushed Lindsey's hair out of her face and

looked down at her. "Growing up doesn't mean giving up on your dreams."

"It did for me," Lindsey said. "I have too many bills to pay. And even if I didn't, the chances of me being able to make a living from my art aren't great. That's the reality of being an artist."

"What kind of art do you make?"

"I draw and paint. Well, I used to. I haven't for a while."

"You don't even do it for fun?" Camilla asked.

"Nope. I don't really feel like it these days." Lindsey shut her eyes. "It was a childish dream anyway."

CHAPTER ELEVEN

"I'm so stuffed," Camilla said. "I can barely move."

Lindsey murmured in agreement. The two of them were sprawled out in the lounge just off the dining room, finishing the bottle of wine they'd opened with dinner. Camilla had recovered from her 'flare-up,' which was what she called those periods where her illness got worse, and she was back to her usual self. In fact, she seemed even livelier than before.

"June should have finished drawing my bath by now." Camilla turned to Lindsey. "Would you like to join me?"

Camilla often disappeared to take long baths before bed. This was the first time she had invited Lindsey to join her nightly ritual. The two of them in the bath together? That could only lead to one thing.

Lindsey's entire body sizzled. That night in the playroom seemed like an eternity ago. Since then, Lindsey and Camilla had barely done more than kiss. It only made Lindsey's desire for her grow. Almost every night, Lindsey would lie awake, alternating between thinking about how good it had felt, and wondering why she felt anything at all.

It shouldn't have been a problem for Lindsey. She'd always been open-minded when it came to all things sex and sexuality. She had no reason to resist what she felt toward Camilla. But this was uncharted, unfamiliar territory. Lindsey had never looked at another woman the way she looked at Camilla, never thought about one the way she thought about Camilla every night.

And she certainly had never wanted to get naked in a bathtub with one.

"Where did you go just now, Lindsey?" Camilla asked.

"Uh, nowhere," Lindsey replied.

"Well, if you're not interested, I'll have to take a bath all by myself." Camilla's voice took on a low, sultry timbre. "It's a pity. I was looking forward to having you in there with me, all naked and dripping wet."

Lindsey swallowed. "I'll take a bath with you, Mistress."

The two of them made their way up to Camilla's bathroom. As soon as Lindsey walked through the door, she was hit with the scent of flowers. It was coming from the enormous tub in the corner which was filled to the brim with milky water covered in a layer of petals. Bubbles propelled by underwater jets rose to the surface, and the air above the bath was thick with steam.

Was this what Camilla's nightly baths were like? No wonder she enjoyed them so much.

Camilla shut the door behind her and sat down on the edge of the bathtub. "Undress," Camilla said. "Then undress me."

"Yes, Mistress!" Lindsey pulled her dress up over her

head and hung it on a hook by the door, then slipped out of her bra and panties. Camilla's piercing eyes watched her the entire time. It only excited Lindsey more.

Once her clothes were hung up neatly, Lindsey returned to where Camilla sat.

Camilla straightened out her legs. "Start with my shoes."

Lindsey removed her Mistress's heels one by one, then placed them carefully to the side. Camilla stood up and turned around. Slowly, Lindsey unzipped Camilla's dress, exposing the golden skin of her back inch by inch. She pulled it off, then peeled away Camilla's bra.

Camilla turned to face her. The sight of her Mistress's near-naked body made Lindsey swoon. Camilla's flawless skin glowed, and her hips and breasts were luscious and full. Lindsey found herself wanting to kiss them, and bury herself in them, and get lost in them for hours on end.

"As much as I appreciate you admiring me, I'd like to get into this bath before it gets cold," Camilla said.

Lindsey snapped out of her trance. "Sorry, Mistress."

She looked down at Camilla's panties. They were made of cream-colored silk. Camilla seemed to love silk. Silk sheets, silk nighties, silk lingerie. And these tiny silk panties that Lindsey had just been instructed to remove.

Lindsey dropped to her knees and pulled Camilla's panties down her hips and all the way to the ground. She barely caught a glimpse of what was underneath them before Camilla turned and stepped into the bath.

Camilla slid down into the steamy water with a satisfied groan. "Hang my things up and come join me."

Lindsey did as she was instructed, then got into the bath in front of Camilla, sitting between her legs. Camilla draped her arms around Lindsey's shoulders, pulling her in close. The bathtub was big enough that the two of them could fit without even touching. But where was the fun in that?

"I'll be going away next week," Camilla said. "For five days or so."

"Where are you going?" Lindsey asked.

"To Seattle for work. I have an event to attend the night before I leave, so I'll be staying in the city then going straight to the airport in the morning. It's a fundraising gala for a library downtown. These things are always so dull, but considering I practically gave them the building, I should probably make an appearance."

"You gave away a building?"

"I sold it for a fraction of what it was worth, so I might as well have," Camilla said. "Anyway, I'm letting you know in case you don't want to be alone in the manor while I'm gone. Some people get lonely in this big, secluded house. I won't be offended if you want to make other arrangements."

"I don't mind," Lindsey said. "I think I'll stay."

"You can always go into the city for a day or two. I'll even get you a hotel room if you want to stay the night. Or, you can invite a friend to come here for a few days."

"That could be fun." Lindsey waved her hands through the cloudy water in front of her, gathering a handful of petals. "Faith has been dying to see the place."

"Oh?" Camila said. "You've been telling her all about the manor? About us?"

"Only a little." Well, it was more than a little. Lindsey told Faith everything. Except for the fact that she and Camilla had slept together.

"It's fine, I don't mind if you talk to her about us. And she's more than welcome to come visit."

"Thanks. I'll ask her." Lindsey slipped a little deeper into the bath. "Mistress?"

"Yes?"

"You've been living in the manor by yourself for a while, haven't you?"

"Ever since my parents passed 15 years ago," Camilla replied. "I often have guests though. Friends, relatives, the occasional lover."

"Do you ever get lonely out here in this big house?" Lindsey asked.

"No. I've always preferred solitude, ever since I was a child. I think that's why I like this place so much. My sister used to think I was a freak because I spent every summer of my childhood hiding in the hedge maze reading books. Or I'd just go in there to get away from the craziness inside the manor. You'd think in a house this big, it would be easier to find some peace and quiet."

Lindsey turned to look at Camilla. "You have a sister?"

"She's ten years older than me," Camilla said. "We don't speak very often."

"Why not?"

"We don't exactly get along." Camilla drew her hands down the front of Lindsey's shoulders. "But my sister is the last person I want to think about when I have a beautiful naked woman in my bathtub."

Camilla's hands slithered down to Lindsey's chest. Lindsey's breath hitched. She couldn't help but feel like Camilla was trying to distract her from their conversation. But

Lindsey wasn't complaining. She'd been turned on since the moment Camilla had commanded her to undress.

"Lie back and let your Mistress take care of you," Camilla said.

Lindsey leaned back against Camilla, sinking into her skin. Camilla's breasts pressed into her back, and the scent of the rose petals mingled with the steam from the bath, making her head spin. Camilla began massaging Lindsey's breasts with her slick, soapy fingers. A flood of heat went through her.

Camilla ran her hands downward, all the way to the insides of Lindsey's thighs. She pulled them apart gently and slipped a finger into Lindsey's slit. Lindsey's mouth fell open in a silent moan.

"Are you wet because we're in the bath?" Camilla asked. "Or are you wet for me?"

"For you, Mistress," Lindsey replied.

"Aren't I lucky?" Camilla glided her finger up and down. "I want you to ask me for permission before you come, okay?"

"Yes, Mistress."

Camilla dragged a finger up to Lindsey's clit, circling it slowly. "I'm having some special items made for you." Camilla's other hand crept back up to Lindsey's breasts. "For both of us. Once they arrive, I'm going to take you into the playroom again. Would you like that?"

"Yes, Mistress," Lindsey whispered.

"I'm looking forward to it. I love toying with this lovely body of yours."

Between Lindsey's legs, Camilla's fingers had gone from

slow and light to hard and fast. The soap-filled water made every touch feel even more sensual.

Lindsey exhaled sharply. It hadn't been long, but she was already close. Her head tipped back onto Camilla's shoulder. Camilla responded by kissing and biting Lindsey's bared neck.

Lindsey shuddered. "Mistress, can I come?"

"Not yet," Camilla said. "And if you do, I'll be very disappointed."

Lindsey groaned and let out a curse.

Camilla withdrew her hand. "Watch your language."

Seriously? Some of Camilla's demands were ridiculous, but Lindsey wasn't about to argue with the woman who had control over her pleasure. "Sorry, Mistress."

Camilla slid her hand back down to stroke Lindsey between her thighs. Lindsey whimpered. Her eyes screwed shut as she focused all her energy on holding back the storm raging within her and keeping herself from going over the edge. Just when she thought she couldn't take anymore, Camilla spoke.

"You may come now."

At once, an eruption went off inside Lindsey. Her cry echoed through the bathroom as she bucked against Camilla. Her Mistress held her in place, her fingers still strumming away until every drop of pleasure had been drained out of Lindsey.

She let out a breath. "Thank you, Mistress."

Camilla continued to caress Lindsey's body, her fingers wandering over Lindsey's skin. She traced her hand along Lindsey's collarbone, skimming the long scar that ran along it.

"Where did this come from?" Camilla asked.

"It's from the car accident," Lindsey replied. "Well, the surgery that came after it. I broke my collarbone." She brought her hand up to touch it. It had healed well, and most of the time, she forgot that it was even there.

"I'm sorry, I didn't mean to bring up something sensitive."

"It's all right," Lindsey said. "I have another one on my thigh. I broke my leg too, among other things."

Camilla took Lindsey's hand. "Turn around."

Lindsey twisted to face her. Camilla guided Lindsey's hand down her stomach.

"Do you feel that scar?" She ran Lindsey's finger over a little dip in Camilla's skin. "It's from surgery for endometriosis. I have three of them."

Lindsey had noticed the three round dimples on Camilla's stomach when undressing her earlier, but she hadn't thought anything of it.

"You see?" Camilla said. "You're not the only one with battle scars."

Lindsey smiled softly. It was nice to know they had that in common. But it wasn't those scars that Lindsey cared about. After her accident, she'd realized that the worst scars were the ones no one could see.

CHAPTER TWELVE

"Have you finished with your breakfast?" Camilla asked. "There's something I need to show you."

Lindsey gulped down the last of her coffee. "All done." She got up and followed Camilla out of the dining room. "Where are we going?"

"You'll see in a moment."

Camilla led Lindsey through the house, walking with purposeful strides. It seemed like whatever she wanted to show Lindsey was of the utmost importance.

Camilla stopped in front of a door. "Here we are. Why don't you have a look inside?"

Lindsey opened the door and entered the room. It was a large, light-filled space, enclosed by glass walls on three sides. The view of the grounds outside was magnificent. The room was set up like an artist studio, and a well-equipped one at that. There were easels, a drawing table, and an assortment of art supplies.

"What is this?" Lindsey asked.

"This is the sunroom," Camilla replied. "At least, it used to be. Now, it's your studio."

Lindsey had visited this room while exploring the day she'd arrived at the manor. Back then, it had been furnished with a lounge and a couple of armchairs. "Where did all this come from?"

"Most of the furniture was in storage in the east wing. The easels, the drawing table—they belonged to my grandmother." Camilla strolled up to the table by the window and ran her hand over the smooth, dark wood. "As for the art supplies, I had them delivered yesterday. I wasn't sure what you'd need, so I asked a friend of mine who's an artist to recommend some basics."

Basics didn't even begin to describe everything in the room. It held everything an artist could ever need. Canvases of all shapes and sizes. Pencils, sketch pads, different types of paints. And all of it was of the finest quality, from all the best brands. Camilla's friend had advised her well.

"I hope this is adequate," Camilla said.

"This is more than adequate. I would have killed for this stuff in art school." Lindsey peered into a box filled with very expensive oil paints. She felt a twinge of guilt.

"What's wrong?"

Lindsey hesitated. "I don't know if I'm going to use it, that's all."

"That's where you're wrong," Camilla said. "I've decided you have it too easy doing nothing all day when I'm working. So you're going to do some work of your own."

"What do you mean?"

"From now on, you're going to spend an hour in here after breakfast every day working on your art."

Lindsey opened her mouth, then shut it again. Was Camilla seriously going to force her to do this? "But-"

Camilla folded her arms across her chest. "This isn't a request."

Heat bubbled up inside Lindsey's stomach. For the first time in as long as she could remember, she felt angry.

"You can't just tell me what to do!" Lindsey said.

"The last time I checked, I've been telling you what to do for weeks now," Camilla replied.

"This is different. This isn't like everything else!"

"Why not?"

Hot tears gathered at the corners of Lindsey's eyes. Why was she suddenly finding it so hard to express herself?

"Apple," she said.

At once, Camilla took Lindsey's hand and drew her to a window seat beside them. "I'm sorry, darling. Are you all right?"

"Yeah," Lindsey grumbled.

"I was trying to help. I thought you needed a little push. But I pushed you too hard, didn't I?"

Lindsey nodded. Her frustration had reduced to a simmer.

"Do you want to talk about it?" Camilla asked. "When we spoke the other night in my room, it was obvious that you didn't really want to give up on your art. I could hear it in your voice. Is something holding you back?"

"It's just that, it used to be so easy," Lindsey said. "I used to have this constant desire to create. I used to find inspiration everywhere I looked. But now, every time I even think about trying to draw, or paint, or anything else, it's like I'm paralyzed. I just… can't."

"Well, my grandmother used to say that creating art is work like anything else. Sure, you need talent and inspiration. But sometimes, you just need to sit down and do it."

"I don't think I can."

"You'll never know if you don't try," Camilla said.

Lindsey frowned in thought. It was true that she hadn't actually tried. She'd told herself that she was too busy, or that there was no point because she was never going to be able to make a living from her art.

But those reasons alone shouldn't have stopped her from doing what she loved. Were they just excuses? As Lindsey looked around the studio, she realized she was avoiding the truth. She was scared. Scared that she'd fail. Scared that she'd lost that innate part of herself that was capable of creating great things.

Scared that the person she was before the accident no longer existed.

"Do you think you can do that for me?" Camilla asked. "Just try? Maybe not this morning, or even today, or tomorrow. But one day, in the time you have left living here with me, will you try to find the joy that art used to bring you?"

Lindsey blinked away her half-formed tears. "Okay," she said quietly. "I'll try. I'll try now." She knew that if she put it off any longer, she'd lose her resolve.

Camilla kissed her gently. "Are you going to be okay?"

"Yes. I will."

"If you're not, come find me in my office. And remember, this room is yours, and yours alone. I'll never come in here without your permission. If you need more supplies or anything specific that you can't find in here, let me know, and I'll get it for you."

Lindsey nodded.

"I'll leave you to it."

Moments later, Lindsey was alone in the room. She felt so overwhelmed. Where should she even start? She hadn't picked up a pencil or a paintbrush since she'd finished her art degree. Did she still have it in her? That passion that fueled her creativity? That sense of wonder about the world around her, and that need to capture it all on a piece of paper or canvas?

Could she ever get that passion back again?

Lindsey didn't have a choice but to try. Camilla had decreed it. Sure, Lindsey didn't really have to listen to her. But she knew that if she didn't, Camilla would be so disappointed.

She gazed out toward the garden just outside. This particular garden was filled with bright, colorful lilies. The sky was clear and the morning sun cast dappled light through the leaves of the nearby trees. As Lindsey looked on, a tiny bird flew down to perch on the edge of a birdbath in the center of the garden.

Seriously? The scene couldn't have been more picturesque. Clearly, it was a sign.

Lindsey glanced over at the desk. On top of it was a sketchpad and an assortment of pencils and boxes of charcoal. She grabbed the sketchpad and a stick of charcoal, pulled a chair over to the window, and sat down.

Taking a deep breath, she put the charcoal to the paper and began to sketch.

Lindsey put her sketchpad down in her lap. It had taken her several attempts, but she'd finally managed to capture the scene before her in a way that she didn't hate. The lighting wasn't right, and the leaves on the trees were nothing more than vague scribbles, but it was a lot better than her first few attempts. The floor around her was littered with crumpled up balls of sketch paper.

Lindsey looked around. She was sure there was a clock in here somewhere. She spotted the old timepiece on the sideboard and gasped. It was 12:30. She'd been in here for hours! And she was late for lunch with Camilla. Lindsey cursed. One of Camilla's rules was to stick to the schedule.

And Lindsey had learned her lesson about breaking Camilla's rules.

She returned her sketchpad to the desk, and dashed out into the hall, heading for the dining room. When she reached it, she almost knocked June over outside the doorway. Lindsey murmured an apology and entered the room.

Camilla was sitting at her place at the table, flicking through a newspaper, her empty plate pushed aside. She looked up at Lindsey. "How nice of you to finally join me."

"I'm sorry, Mistress!" Lindsey said. "I lost track of time. I was working on a sketch."

"In that case, I'll let it slide." Camilla pushed out the chair next to her. "Sit. June will bring you lunch."

Lindsey sat down, her stomach rumbling. She hadn't realized how hungry she was. Almost immediately, June appeared and set down a plate of sandwiches before Lindsey, then disappeared again. Lindsey began to wolf them down.

"I take it you were enjoying yourself?" Camilla asked.

"I don't know if enjoying is the right word," Lindsey said. "It was difficult. And frustrating. It was like I'd forgotten everything I'd ever learned. But after a while, it all came back to me." A smile spread across her face. "God, I'd forgotten what that felt like. To get so lost in something that it's like the rest of the world just fades away. It's a great feeling."

"I'm happy for you," Camilla said. "And I'm proud of you."

A warm flush washed over her. "You were right. I just needed a little push."

After a few more minutes of conversation, Camilla got up and placed her hand on Lindsey's forearm. "I have to go make a few work calls. But once you're done with lunch, come find me in the library and we can spend a bit of time together. Unfortunately, I need to get some work done, but I can do it with you there."

"Okay, Mistress."

Lindsey finished off her lunch, then left the dining room, nearly barreling June over for the second time. She apologized again, then headed to the library. She didn't know why she was in such a hurry. The events of the morning had filled her with nervous energy.

Lindsey knocked on the door.

"Come in," Camilla said.

Lindsey entered the library. It was one of the smaller rooms in the house, consisting of little more than a desk and two armchairs. But every inch of the walls, from the floor to the high ceiling, was covered in shelves packed with books. A tall ladder on wheels leaned against one wall.

Camilla was seated in the armchair flicking through

some papers. She looked up at Lindsey. "I hope you didn't have trouble finding this place."

"I've been in here before," Lindsey said. "It's pretty impressive."

"This was my mother's library. I like to come here to work when I feel like a change of scenery. You're welcome to borrow any of the books. My mother's collection is quite large and varied."

"Okay. Thanks, Mistress."

Camilla gestured toward the floor by her feet, where a thick velvet cushion lay. "Come sit with me."

Lindsey walked over to her and sat down on the cushion, her legs out to the side. After a moment, she leaned her head against Camilla's legs.

Camilla's hand dropped down to stroke the top of Lindsey's head. "You know, I'd love to see your art someday. That is, if you ever feel comfortable showing it to me."

"Sure," Lindsey said. "It might be a while until I have anything worth showing you, though. I'm out of practice."

"That's okay. Whenever you're ready."

They lapsed into silence. For a few minutes, the only sounds were the scratching of Camilla's pen and the occasional murmur from Camilla.

Lindsey looked up at her. "Mistress? Can I ask you some questions?"

"You can ask me whatever you like," Camilla said, her focus still on her work. "I might even answer you."

"Well, when you told me about endometriosis, you said to look it up. And I did, but it was all medical stuff. I guess I was wondering what living with it is like for you?"

"Well, it isn't the most glamorous of illnesses," Camilla

said. "It's like having horrendous period cramps while constantly feeling exhausted and awful in general. Most of the time it's manageable, but sometimes, it can floor me for days, or even weeks. You've seen how bad it can get for yourself. Mine is a relatively severe case though."

"But, isn't there anything you can do about it?" Lindsey asked. "Doctors? Medications? Treatments?"

"Trust me, I've seen the finest specialists in the country, and I've had every possible treatment. But the reality is that there's a lot that medical science doesn't know how to fix. Endometriosis is one of those things. There are little things that help, but nothing that is actually going to cure me."

"That sucks." Lindsey couldn't think of anything to say that didn't sound inadequate. "I know you said not to feel sorry for you, but it just seems so unfair."

"It does make things hard." Camilla paused to study something on the page in front of her. "But, as I said, I've been dealt a good hand otherwise. I have this house and a job that allows me to have a lot of flexibility, with me being the boss and all. And I don't even need to work. I could live off my inheritance if I wanted to. But I don't want that. My family's company means a lot to me, so I'd rather work, even if it means sacrificing other things."

"Like… relationships?" Lindsey asked.

"I have a few close friends. They're all I need."

"But, don't you want to find love?" Lindsey's question sounded childish, even to her.

"It's just not a priority for me," Camilla said. "I don't have the time or patience for dating anymore. Besides, I've worked hard to build this life for myself. Adding another person to it complicates things. And I don't like change."

Lindsey wasn't surprised that Camilla considered a relationship a 'complication.' She knew how much her Mistress hated any disruptions to her carefully organized life.

"That's not to say I'm not open to love. If the perfect woman turned up on my doorstep, I wouldn't turn her away." Camilla patted Lindsey's head, then grabbed a pen from the table next to her and began to scribble on the document she was holding.

It was clear that she was done answering questions. But Lindsey still had something she wanted to ask her Mistress. "What about…"

"Yes?" Camilla said.

"What about sex?"

"What about it?"

"Well, I read that for women with endometriosis sex can be… hard."

"Yes, it can be for me under some circumstances. But I can still enjoy it. It just requires a lot of care. That's why I prefer to take the reins, so to speak."

"Is that why you're a Domme?" Lindsey asked.

Camilla thought for a moment. "I suppose it is, in a way. But not in the way you think." She put her pen and paper down in her lap. "My illness can be unpredictable at times. Sure, there are patterns, but I never really know when it's going to flare up. When you're dealing with a condition that has a lot of ups and downs, it's easy to feel like you're not in control of your own body, let alone your own life. It can be liberating to take that control back."

"That makes sense," Lindsey said.

"Of course, there are other reasons why I like being a dominant." Camilla drew the back of her finger up the side of Lindsey's cheek. Her voice dropped low. "There's something addictive about making a submissive squirm."

A flicker of lust ran down Lindsey's spine. Camilla sure knew how to make her squirm.

"Now, as much as I enjoy your presence, I should get back to work. Why don't you go take advantage of this lovely afternoon?"

"Okay, Mistress."

Lindsey stood up and shook out her numb legs. She had pushed Camilla far enough out of her comfort zone for the day.

Before leaving the room, Lindsey paused by the door. "Thank you," she said.

"For what?" Camilla asked.

"For pushing me this morning. I needed that."

Camilla gave her a half smile. "I'll see you at dinner. Try not to be late this time."

CHAPTER THIRTEEN

"Lindsey?" June appeared in the doorway of the sitting room. "Faith has arrived."

Lindsey thanked June and made her way downstairs. It was Friday evening. Camilla had left for her trip several days ago, and she was due back tomorrow night. Lindsey had spent most of the week enjoying the solitude of the grounds. But Camilla had been right. Lindsey was starting to feel lonely, so she was looking forward to having Faith around, even if it was just for one night.

By the time Lindsey reached the front door, Faith had hopped out of the car.

She spotted Lindsey and waved. "Wow, you weren't kidding about this place. It's huge."

"Yep." Lindsey pulled Faith in for a hug. She'd actually forgotten how awesome the manor was. After living here for a month, it had become normal. Going back to the real world was going to be a rude shock. "What do you want to do first? I can show you around?"

"Sure," Faith said. "Let's start with your room. I want to see all the stuff Camilla bought you."

A few minutes and a greeting from June later, they were in Lindsey's bedroom. Lindsey sat on the bed while Faith flicked through her wardrobe, squealing with excitement every now and then.

"If Camilla wants another sugar baby, I volunteer," Faith said. "You get to keep all this?"

"Yep," Lindsey replied.

Faith pulled out a long evening gown that Lindsey hadn't even worn yet. "This would fetch a great price online."

Lindsey hadn't even thought about that. She'd barely thought about her money problems since she moved in. As promised, Camilla had deposited a generous allowance into Lindsey's bank account every week since she'd arrived, but it wasn't like she needed it. She had everything she needed here at the manor, and Camilla provided whatever Lindsey asked for. She'd practically forgotten that money was a part of the arrangement.

Faith hung the dress back up and joined Lindsey on the bed. "So, you're getting paid to live in this huge mansion. You're getting all this free stuff. And all you have to do is keep some rich woman company?"

"Pretty much," Lindsey replied. "But Camilla isn't 'some rich woman.' She's Camilla. She's pretty incredible." She glanced sideways at her friend. "Besides, we've been doing more than just keeping each other company."

Faith's eyes widened. "Are you saying you've been sleeping with her?"

"Only a couple of times." Even though that particular

box had been opened, their relationship was still more about their routine, day-to-day power games than sex.

"And? Did you like it?"

Lindsey nodded. "A lot, actually. And I like her a lot."

"Wow," Faith said. "It sounds like this arrangement is really working out for you."

"Yeah. It is." Lindsey's phone started to ring. She glanced at the screen. "It's Camilla. I should take this."

"Go ahead." Faith grinned. "I'm sure you don't want to keep her waiting."

Lindsey ignored Faith's comment and picked up the phone. "Hi, Camilla."

"*Camilla?* That's no way to address your Mistress." There was a sultry edge to Camilla's voice. "Do I need to get out the cane?"

Heat rushed to Lindsey's face. Not to mention other places. She got up from the bed as casually as she could and turned away to look out the window so Faith couldn't see her bright red face.

"Well?" Camilla said.

"Um, I'm hanging out with Faith at the moment."

"Oh? And you're too shy to call me Mistress in front of her?"

"Yes," Lindsey said.

"If you ask me nicely, I might let it slide," Camilla said.

Seriously? Lindsey peered over her shoulder at Faith, who wasn't even pretending not to eavesdrop. "Please?" she mumbled.

"Well that didn't sound sincere at all. I know what you sound like when you beg for real."

A sharp, faint breath escaped from Lindsey's mouth. She

clamped her lips shut and stared even more intently out the window, trying not to think about the images Camilla's words conjured up.

"Nevertheless, I'm a generous Mistress. I'll let it go just this once."

"Thank you," Lindsey said.

"Tell Faith I said hello, and to make herself at home."

"I will." Lindsey looked back at Faith, who was sprawled out on the bed. "I should warn you, she's already five minutes away from moving in."

Faith stuck out her tongue.

"Well, she's welcome to stay for a few days if you'd like," Camilla said. "Speaking of which, I have some bad news. I have a lot more to do here than I expected, so I'm going to have to stay a bit longer. I won't be back until Tuesday."

"Oh," Lindsey said. "That's okay."

"Let me make it up to you. I've booked a reservation at my favorite day spa in the city for you and Faith. I hope you don't already have plans tomorrow?"

"No, we don't. Thank you!"

"It's my pleasure. But you're going to have to do something for me too." Camilla's voice took on that serious tone she always used when she made demands. "There's a credit card in the top drawer of the desk in my study. I want you to take it with you when you go into the city tomorrow and buy something to wear the night that I come back."

"What kind of something?" Lindsey asked.

"A dress, and some other pieces. There are several boutiques downtown that I frequent. I'll send you their details, as well as some suggestions. Just mention my name, and they'll help you pick out something appropriate. We'll be having a dinner date in the garden. And after dinner, we'll see where the night takes us. Maybe we'll have dessert in the playroom again."

Lindsey felt a throb of desire. "Okay," she said. But 'Yes, Mistress' was what she really meant.

"I look forward to seeing what you pick out for me."

Lindsey hung up the phone and turned back around. Faith was still stretched out on the bed, smiling.

"What?" Lindsey asked.

"Nothing," Faith replied. "What did Camilla want?"

"She's staying in Seattle for a few more days. She's booked a spa day for us as an apology." Lindsey fell down onto the bed next to her friend. "And, we're going shopping."

Lindsey slipped her jeans back on and pulled her blouse over her head, then flattened down her hair in the dressing room mirror. She and Faith only had ten minutes before their spa appointment. They'd been shopping all morning at Camilla's boutiques of choice. The 'suggestions' Camilla sent Lindsey ended up being a set of specific instructions on what to buy.

It was typical of Camilla. Even when asking Lindsey to pick out something herself, Camilla was still pulling the strings. Lindsey didn't mind. She was doing this for her Mistress, after all.

Besides, Lindsey had decided to get a little something to complete the outfit. Something that would really surprise Camilla.

She opened the curtain and joined Faith outside the dressing room.

"What did you decide on?" Faith asked.

Lindsey held up a baby blue bra and panty set made of silk and lace. It cost a fortune, but Camilla was paying for it. Camilla hadn't actually told Lindsey to buy lingerie. Lindsey hoped that Camilla would be pleased by the gesture rather than angry at Lindsey for acting without her Mistress's express permission.

Her Mistress. This wasn't the first time Lindsey had thought of Camilla as 'her Mistress' rather than just 'Camilla.' It was happening more and more lately, and it did little to help with Lindsey's confusion about her feelings. It was ironic, really. Lindsey had gone into this faking attraction to Camilla and even faking her sexuality.

But right now, everything felt very real.

"Earth to Lindsey," Faith said.

"Right," Lindsey pulled herself together. "Let's go pay for this."

"Hold on. Is something the matter?"

"I don't know." Lindsey sighed. "It's just that, this whole sugar baby thing was just supposed to be a way to make some money. And then when I met Camilla, we really clicked, and I thought, maybe this could be fun. But now that we've gotten closer, and we're having mind-blowing sex, I've started having all these feelings about her. What does that mean?"

"It doesn't have to mean anything," Faith said. "So you're into Camilla. It's not like you have to slap a rainbow bumper sticker on your car now."

"It's not that simple. I know it is for you, but it isn't for me. I've never been anything other than straight. And if I do have feelings for Camilla, what does that make me?"

"Does it matter? Attraction isn't always black and white. Everyone's experience is different. Maybe you like women. Maybe you just like sex with women. Maybe you just like sex with Camilla. Or maybe, you just like her, period. You don't have to put a label on whatever it is you feel."

"But I don't even know what it is I feel toward her. For starters, I can't figure out whether I'm attracted to her dominant side, or if it's really her that I'm attracted to."

"Aren't they the same thing?" Faith asked. "Isn't her dominant side just a part of her?"

"I guess." After all, Lindsey's submissive side was a part of her too. "But I don't know if my feelings are because we've been doing all these intimate things together and I'm mistaking that closeness for something else. And I don't know whether my attraction to her is romantic, or if I'm just getting caught up in this lie that we're living together. I've never felt anything like this toward another woman before. How am I supposed to know if it's real or not?"

"I don't know," Faith said. "But maybe it would be easier to figure out the answers to these questions if your feelings for Camilla weren't all wrapped up in your ideas about yourself. It sounds like you're trying to come to terms with the fact that maybe your sexuality isn't what you think it is while trying to work out how you feel toward Camilla at the same time." She squeezed Lindsey's arm. "Stop worrying about what you think you should or shouldn't feel, and just let yourself feel it."

Was it really that easy? Could Lindsey just let go of everything she knew about herself and embrace her feelings for Camilla? That undeniable pull she felt whenever she was in her Mistress's presence? That insatiable need to please her? The electric charge that went through Lindsey's body whenever Camilla touched her?

And was there really any point in doing that when everything between them was pretend?

CHAPTER FOURTEEN

Lindsey looked at the time. 10 p.m. Camilla was supposed to have arrived at the manor before dinner, but she'd messaged Lindsey a few hours ago to tell her that her flight was delayed. She was due home any minute now, but it was too late for dinner. Lindsey was a little disappointed. She'd been looking forward to spending the evening with Camilla. It seemed silly how much she missed Camilla, considering she'd only been away for a week or so. But they'd been living together for over a month now. Lindsey had gotten so used to her constant presence.

She looked out her bedroom window. There were two pinpricks of light in the distance. They had to be the headlights of a car coming up the long driveway. Lindsey rushed to the mirror and looked at herself. She'd put on the knee-length strapless dress she'd bought on the weekend before receiving Camilla's message. Now, the lightweight fabric was full of wrinkles, and the tie around the waist was loose.

Lindsey retied the belt, smoothed out the creases in the skirt, and headed downstairs.

By the time Lindsey reached the entrance hall, Camilla was walking through the door, a small suitcase trailing behind her. She spotted Lindsey.

"Lindsey." Camilla's voice echoed through the hall. "I'm so sorry for keeping you waiting."

Lindsey's heart began to pound. Just the sight of Camilla filled her with longing. She remembered what Faith had told her. *Stop worrying about what you think you should or shouldn't feel, and just let yourself feel it.*

Completely unprompted, Lindsey's feet carried her to the door where her Mistress stood. She threw her arms around Camilla's neck and kissed her urgently, as if they'd been apart for months, not days.

Camilla broke away. "What was that for?"

"I missed you, Mistress," Lindsey replied.

"I can tell. I missed you too, darling. Let me look at you."

Lindsey took a step back and did a twirl.

"You look beautiful. I love the dress you picked out." Camilla looked down at her own wrinkled blouse and slacks. "I wish I weren't so under-dressed. You went to all this effort, and I missed our dinner."

"It's okay," Lindsey said. "I'm just glad you're back."

A smile danced on Camilla's lips. "If it's not too late for you, we could still have dessert in the playroom."

"No, it's not too late." Lindsey trailed her fingers up Camilla's arm. "But how about we skip the dessert part?"

"That's a wonderful idea." Camilla's voice dropped to a whisper. "My special delivery is waiting for us in the playroom. I can't wait to try it out."

Camilla took Lindsey's hand and dragged her upstairs. As they passed through the white double doors leading to Camilla's rooms, June called out Camilla's name from behind them.

"You're back," she said. "Is there anything you need, Ma'am?"

"No, June," Camilla said impatiently. "I appreciate you waiting up for me, but you can go to bed."

"All right. Good night, Ma'am. Good night, Lindsey." June gave Lindsey a polite nod before scurrying off.

When they finally reached the playroom, Camilla pulled Lindsey inside. Like last time, everything was hidden away in drawers and cabinets. However, there was a small wooden chest sitting in the center of the table.

Camilla spoke into Lindsey's ear. "I'm glad you wanted to skip dessert, because I'm going to do all kinds of dirty things to you on that table."

Lindsey sucked in a breath. Her Mistress knew exactly which buttons to push. She led Lindsey over to the table and gestured for her to sit on top of it. Lindsey glanced down at the chest on the tabletop next to her. It was made of dark wood, and it was held shut by a small gold padlock. Etched into the lid in gold calligraphy were the letters 'C.R.' Camilla's initials.

Camilla ran her fingertips over the lid of the chest. "I have a friend who does incredible work with leather. I asked her to make some items for us." She slid the wooden box to the side, away from Lindsey. "No peeking. It's a surprise."

Camilla unlocked the chest and opened it up, the lid blocking Lindsey's view. She reached inside and pulled out a set of interconnected straps made of dark blue leather. Before Lindsey could try to work out what they were for, Camilla placed them on the table, reached into the box again, and produced a pair of leather cuffs. They were the same midnight blue color, with contrasting gold buckles and O-rings. The cuffs were embossed with an intricate design.

"There's more, but I'll save the rest for another time." Camilla shut the lid. "Hold out your arms."

Lindsey presented her wrists. Camilla buckled a cuff around one wrist, then the other.

"There," Camilla said. "Do you like them?"

"I love them." Lindsey held her hands up in front of her, inspecting the cuffs. "They're beautiful."

"They're a real work of art. Look at them closely."

Lindsey examined the cuffs. The buckles and O-rings looked like they were made of real gold. And hanging from each of the O-rings was a small, round tag engraved with the same letters that were on the lid of the box. Lindsey read them out loud. "C.R."

"My initials," Camilla said. "You're all mine now. You'll wear these whenever we're in here."

Lindsey's stomach fluttered. "Thank you, Mistress."

Camilla drew her close and pressed her lips against Lindsey's. The kiss rippled through Lindsey's body. Her Mistress pushed herself between Lindsey's knees and slid a hand up the front of her thigh. Lindsey's dress bunched up around her hips. She held onto the edge of the table, steadying herself against Camilla's dizzying passion.

"These cuffs aren't just for show," Camilla said. "We're

going to test them out. But first, let's get you out of that dress."

Camilla pulled Lindsey off the table and untied the belt around her waist. She turned around for Camilla to unzip it at the back. Why had she chosen such a fiddly dress?

Camilla tugged at the zipper. An irritated growl emerged from her chest.

Lindsey peered over her shoulder. "Is it stuck?"

"Yes," Camilla said. "But it's an easy problem to solve."

Without hesitation, Camilla grabbed the top of the dress with both hands and tore it down the seam next to the zipper. The strapless dress fell down around Lindsey's hips.

Lindsey gasped. Camilla had just destroyed the absurdly expensive dress that Lindsey had spent half of Saturday picking out. But Camilla had paid for it after all. It was hers. Lindsey was hers.

And nothing turned Lindsey on more.

She spun back around to find her Mistress's eyes filled with fire. A thrill went through Lindsey's body. Camilla wanted her. To own her, to possess her, to make Lindsey hers. She tugged Lindsey's dress all the way down to the floor, then tore off her own blouse and slacks. Then she drew Lindsey in and smothered her with her lips. Her hands traveled up the side of Lindsey's chest to cradle her breast through her thin silk bra.

"Wait," Camilla pulled back and looked Lindsey up and down, her eyes lingering on the pale blue bra and panties Lindsey wore. "Where did you get these?"

The lingerie. Lindsey had been so caught up in the moment that she'd forgotten all about it. "I bought them for you."

"Did you now?" Camilla scrutinized her silently.

"They're a gift for you, Mistress," Lindsey said. "Do you like them?"

Camilla walked around Lindsey in a circle, inspecting her from every angle. "I do like them. You look good enough to eat." She backed Lindsey against the table slowly. "It's a pity I'm going to have to take it all off."

Camilla unclipped Lindsey's bra and tossed it aside, then drew a hand up Lindsey's bare chest. Her other hand slid down to Lindsey's silk panties, which were already wet. Lindsey shivered.

Camilla slipped a finger into the side of Lindsey's panties, fingering her slit. "Do you want your Mistress to fuck you?"

"God, yes." Lindsey hadn't forgotten that Camilla had forbidden her from cursing, but apparently, the rule didn't apply to Camilla. Lindsey wasn't about to argue. Hearing her prim and proper Mistress talk dirty was hot as hell.

Camilla stepped back. "Bend over the table and raise your arms up to the corners."

Lindsey did as her Mistress instructed. The solid wood of the tabletop felt cold against her breasts. Those puzzling leather straps that matched the cuffs on Lindsey's wrists were still sitting on the table in front of her.

Camilla walked over to a cabinet and pulled out two short coils of rope. One by one, she looped a length of rope through the gold ring on each of Lindsey's cuffs and tied them in place. Then she took the other ends of the ropes and tied them around the legs of the table where they met the tabletop.

Lindsey was left bound to the table, bent at the waist, her

ass sticking out. The ropes had some give, but it wasn't enough for her to stand or change position. All she could do was wait patiently for her Mistress to give her what she desperately needed.

Camilla picked up the tangle of leather straps from the table and held them up. "Now is the perfect time to test this out."

Lindsey stared at the straps. They looked like some kind of harness. And there was a large gold ring at the front of it all.

Oh. *Oh.*

Lindsey was pretty experienced when it came to sex. But this was one thing she'd never tried, for obvious reasons.

Camilla headed for a set of drawers by the bed, stripping off her bra and panties as she walked. She opened up a drawer and produced a clear glass dildo. With great care, she threaded it through the gold ring, stepped into the straps, and fastened the whole contraption around her hips, before returning to Lindsey's side.

Lindsey was surprised by how well Camilla wore the strap-on. It seemed natural, like an extension of her body. With every movement she made, it bobbed and swayed with her.

"Are you ready for me?" Camilla asked.

"I'm so ready, Mistress." The other times they'd had sex had been tender and gentle. But after spending a week apart, Lindsey wanted nothing more than for her Mistress to take her and claim her as her own.

Camilla rounded the table behind Lindsey, grabbed the waistband of her panties, and pulled them down to the floor. Lindsey pushed them aside with a foot and spread her feet apart. Camilla slid a hand down Lindsey's slit, stroking her silken folds.

"You really are ready," Camilla said. "Have you been dripping wet this whole time, waiting for me?"

Lindsey's answer was a moan.

Camilla wrapped her fingers around Lindsey's hair, pulling her head up. She leaned down to speak into Lindsey's ear. "That's no way to speak to your Mistress."

"Yes, Mistress," Lindsey said. "I've been waiting for you."

"I'm glad. Because I've been waiting to do this to you too."

Lindsey spread her legs out wider. She ached for Camilla. Again, she felt Camilla probe between her lips. But this time, it was the solid glass head of the strap-on. Lindsey's breath quickened.

Finally, Camilla grabbed onto Lindsey's waist with one hand and entered her. Lindsey's mouth fell open in a silent cry. She clutched the sides of the table, holding on as Camilla thrust in and out, sending surges of pleasure through her.

"Mistress…" *Harder*, Lindsey wanted to say. *Faster.* Instead, she closed her eyes and surrendered to her Mistress's control. Camilla plunged deeper, each stroke nudging that sensitive spot inside. And when Camilla's fingers laced around Lindsey's hair again, she lost the ability to form words altogether.

Moments later, an orgasm hit her hard and fast. Lindsey jerked against her restraints, her body racked with tremors, as Camilla buried herself inside her. Then she slumped down on the table, overcome.

Camilla rounded the table and kissed Lindsey softly.

After removing the strap-on, she untied the ropes binding Lindsey to the table but left the cuffs fastened around her wrists. Together, they made their way over to the bed and collapsed onto it.

"Mistress?" Lindsey said breathlessly.

"Yes?"

"I really liked that dress."

Camilla laughed. "I'll buy you another. I'll buy you ten dresses. I'll buy you anything you want." She cupped Lindsey's cheeks and kissed her.

As Lindsey lost herself in Camilla's lips, she realized that it wasn't pretty dresses, or fancy dinners, or expensive gifts that she wanted. What she wanted was Camilla, in every way she could possibly want another person.

She and her Mistress had built this irresistible lie together. And Lindsey was starting to find it hard to separate the lie from the truth.

CHAPTER FIFTEEN

*L*indsey dove into the pool and swam to the other end in one breath. She surfaced, pushed her wet hair out of her eyes and looked over at the deck. Camilla was lounging on a chair in sunglasses and a wide-brimmed hat. She had a stylish one piece on under her wrap, but it was clear that she had no intention of getting into the pool. Even though it was just after lunch, and Camilla wasn't supposed to be working, she'd spent the last fifteen minutes sending emails on her phone.

Lindsey swam over to the edge of the pool. "Mistress?"

"Yes, Lindsey?" Camilla murmured.

"Want to join me in here?"

Camilla peered over her sunglasses, her eyes rolling down Lindsey's bikini-clad body. The bikini Camilla had bought her, of course. "Why should I get in there, when I have this lovely view from here?"

"Because this pool would be a lot more fun with you in it."

"Believe me, I'm tempted. But we both know what's

going to happen if I get in there with you. And I have far too much to do right now to be distracted."

Camilla had seemed busier than usual with work in the past couple of days. And she seemed a little stressed about it.

Maybe Lindsey could do something to help. "Can I come sit with you, Mistress?"

"Sure," Camilla said. "Dry yourself off first. I don't want water on this wrap."

Lindsey swam to the steps and hopped out of the pool. After drying off, she spread her towel out next to Camilla's chair and sat down on it, resting her head against the side of Camilla's thigh. She could have just sat in the chair at the other side of Camilla instead of on the ground. But Lindsey's small gestures of submission always seemed to please her Mistress. Maybe it would help her relax a little.

Camilla's hand dropped down to caress the side of Lindsey's face, while her other hand typed away on her phone. "How would you feel about having some friends of mine come visit?"

"Sure," Lindsey said. What would Camilla's friends be like? And what would Camilla say to them about Lindsey? Would she tell the truth about their unconventional arrangement?

"Maybe I'll throw a dinner party. It's been a while since I hosted one."

"That sounds like fun." Lindsey closed her eyes, letting the warm sun beat down on her skin. This was the life. Luxuriating by the pool next to a mansion, with her beautiful Mistress next to her.

Lindsey never imagined herself in this situation. But

what was more unexpected were her feelings toward Camilla. She'd taken Faith's advice and stopped worrying about what those feelings meant. It had made things a little clearer. But that still left her with one problem.

Everything between Lindsey and Camilla was just a lie.

Camilla yawned. "How's your art going? Do you have anything to show me yet?"

"Not yet," Lindsey replied. "Soon, though." She was out of practice, both in terms of her craft and mentally. It was still a daily battle to sit down and force herself to work every morning. She still felt that paralyzing fear. But it was nowhere near as bad as before. And once she got started, creativity would flow from her for hours and hours.

"June said you've been wandering around with your sketchpad of a morning."

"I've been sketching the grounds. There's so much beautiful scenery here. I don't usually draw landscapes, but the grounds are too picturesque not to try to capture."

"My grandmother spent most of her retirement painting the grounds," Camilla said. "She was very talented. Her paintings are stashed away in the east wing somewhere if you'd like to see them. I'll have June dig them out for you."

"That sounds like a lot of trouble," Lindsey said. "I don't want to make more work for June."

"Nonsense. I pay her outrageously so that I can ask her to do whatever I need done. She won't mind."

"Then I'd love to see them. Thank you, Mistress."

Camilla placed her phone down on the table next to her. "All right. Get up here." She held out her hand and pulled Lindsey up onto her lap. "I can't get anything done with you sitting there. You're much too distracting."

Lindsey grinned. "Sorry, Mistress."

"You're not sorry at all, are you?"

Lindsey threw her arms around Camilla's neck. "No, Mistress, I'm not."

Camilla's mouth fell open. "What has gotten into you today? I ought to take you into the hedge maze where no one can find us and punish you."

"Please do, Mistress." Lindsey was pushing it. Camilla had made it clear in the past that she didn't like misbehaving submissives. But her playful tone suggested that the kind of punishment she was referring to didn't involve writing lines.

"Oh, you're being such a brat right now." Camilla grabbed Lindsey's waist and pulled her closer. "Luckily, I know just how to stop you running that mouth of yours."

Camilla covered Lindsey's mouth with her own, kissing her in that soft, slow way that filled Lindsey with need. She shifted on Camilla's lap, pressing herself against the other woman. Camilla's hand slid up the side of Lindsey's hip, all the way to her chest. A faint moan escaped Lindsey's lips. She really hoped Camilla's talk of taking her into the hedge maze wasn't just a threat.

"Who the hell is this?"

Camilla tensed. Lindsey's eyes flew open. She turned to see a short middle-aged woman standing right beside them. Several feet behind her, June was hurrying toward them, an apologetic look on her face.

"Denise?" Camilla said. "What are you doing here?"

"What do you think?" the woman replied. "I'm visiting my baby sister."

This was Camilla's sister? They did look alike. Both

women had the same hazel eyes and straight brown hair, although Denise's was cut into a short bob. And Denise's face had none of Camilla's warmth and humor.

Denise narrowed her eyes at Lindsey. "I wasn't aware you had a guest, Millie."

Lindsey remembered she was still sitting in Camilla's lap, her hand hovering dangerously close to Camilla's breast. And she was fairly sure Denise had seen them making out like horny teenagers only moments ago. She jumped to her feet.

The motion seemed to break Camilla out of her shocked state. "Lindsey, this is my sister, Denise. Denise, this is Lindsey. My… girlfriend."

Girlfriend? "Uh, hi." Lindsey held her hand out to Denise.

Denise ignored it. Instead, she looked Lindsey up and down, her nose wrinkled in disdain. "She certainly has the 'girl' part down."

Lindsey folded her arms across her chest. Suddenly, she felt very naked in her bikini.

"Lindsey, darling, you'll have to forgive my sister. She isn't normally this rude." Camilla shot Denise a withering look. "Oh, who am I kidding? Yes, she is."

The other woman didn't react. "I didn't know you were seeing someone."

"It's a recent development. Now, I'm sure you're tired after your flight. I'll have June make up one of the guest suites. Why don't you go relax in the drawing room? June can show you the way."

"I grew up in this house. I know where the drawing room is."

"Well, it's been so long since you've been here that I thought you might have forgotten."

"It hasn't been that long." Denise rolled her eyes. "I'm going to go freshen up, then catch up on some work. I'll come down for dinner." She turned to address June. "Seven thirty, in the formal dining room."

"June isn't a servant," Camilla said. "And she doesn't take instructions from you. Dinner will be in the west dining room, as usual. And it will be at seven thirty because it's always at seven thirty."

"Whatever you say, Millie."

"It's *Camilla*. It's been Camilla since I was sixteen."

And if Lindsey hadn't known better, she'd think the pair of them were sixteen. They sure were acting like it.

"I don't have time for this. If you need me, I'll be in my rooms." Denise turned on her heel and stormed back to the house.

As soon as she was out of earshot, Camilla turned to June, a dark look in her eyes. "Why didn't you warn me she was here?"

"I'm sorry, Ma'am," June said. "I was tidying up in the east wing. I didn't hear her arrive."

"Just go make sure she stays away from my rooms. And lock the playroom door for me. You know how she is about that kind of thing."

June nodded, then strode off after Denise.

Camilla turned to Lindsey. "I'm sorry for putting you on the spot like that. Denise would never approve of our arrangement."

"It's okay," Lindsey said.

"Of course, if you're not comfortable with me

pretending you're my girlfriend, I can think of something else."

"No, I don't mind." It wouldn't be any different to what they were already doing. Although, Lindsey was going to have to remember not to call Camilla 'Mistress.'

"Thank you." The relief was clear on Camilla's face. "Do you mind sleeping in my room for now? You can keep your own rooms for when you need your own space, of course."

"Sure." All this, just to fool Camilla's sister? Lindsey had never seen Camilla so frazzled. "Are you okay?" Lindsey asked.

"It's just my sister. She's the only family I have left, but we don't see eye to eye." Camilla rubbed the back of her neck. "She's a senator like my father was, and we have completely different views on everything. She's never approved of the life I live. I had to come out to her three times until she took me seriously. Then it took another two years before she stopped referring to my girlfriends as 'friends,' and-" Camilla blinked. "I'm rambling. None of that is important. What matters, is that she never stays long. We'll only have to play these roles for a day or two."

CHAPTER SIXTEEN

"I'm staying for a week," Denise said.

Camilla paused, her fork halfway up to her mouth. "A whole week?"

Lindsey focused intently on the food on her plate. Dinner had just started, but the air was already thick with tension. Denise didn't seem to like the fact that Camilla was sitting at the head of the table, and just minutes ago, the two sisters had gotten into an argument because Denise had ordered June to set the table 'the right way.'

Not to mention that Denise had been giving Lindsey dirty looks the entire time.

"Is that a problem?" Denise asked.

"Well, I was planning on throwing a dinner party, but it can wait," Camilla said.

"Oh, don't let me stop you from throwing one of your little parties."

"It's fine. I wouldn't want to cut into our quality time together." Camilla paused. "As much as I enjoy spending time with my dear sister, I have to ask. Isn't campaign season starting soon? Shouldn't you be out there making false promises to the masses?"

"That's why I've come here," Denise said. "I'll be extremely busy from now on, so it'll be my last chance to visit the house in a while."

"How thoughtful of you to see me one last time before you disappear for several years again."

"Stop being so dramatic, Millie. It hasn't been years."

"You're right," Camilla said. "It hasn't been years. Not this time, anyway."

Denise sighed. "When are you going to let that go?"

"Let it go? Our mother had just died, and you were nowhere to be found!"

"We all grieve in different ways. I came back for her funeral, didn't I? Besides, I was busy. I had a family of my own to raise."

"Let's not pretend you actually raised the twins. We both know that the nanny did all the work before you shipped them off to boarding school."

Lindsey glanced at Denise. Her brows were bunched up and her jaw was set. Camilla had hit a nerve.

"I'm fairly certain your kids talk to me more than they do you," Camilla said. "Did you know that your daughter was chosen as captain of her school debate team?"

Denise frowned. "I'm sure she mentioned it in one of her emails."

"She told me when we spoke on the phone last week."

"Yes, well I'm not surprised she talks to you more than me. You're her fun Aunt Camilla. Of course, you can be as eccentric as you like. It must be nice, not having any responsibilities."

"No responsibilities? Who do you think has been running our family's company for the last 15 years while you're off playing politician? Not to mention taking care of this estate. It's funny how you're out there preaching about family and using the Robinson name to get ahead, but when it comes to your own family, you might as well be a ghost."

Lindsey picked up her glass of water, somehow knocking her fork off the table in the process. It fell to the floor, landing with a loud clatter. Denise and Camilla turned to stare at her.

"Er…"

From nowhere, June swooped in and picked the fork up from the floor. "I'll get you a new one." She gave Lindsey a sympathetic look. Something told her that June was used to these dinners with Camilla and Denise.

For a while, only silence filled the air.

Then, Denise cleared her throat. "So, Lindsey, how long have you been living in my family's home?"

"Er, a little over a month." Lindsey and Camilla hadn't discussed what they were going to say to Denise, so Lindsey decided to tell as much of the truth as she could.

Denise huffed. "And how long were the two of you together before you moved in?"

"Denise, that's no way to treat my guest." Camilla put her hand on Lindsey's. "As you can see, I got the looks and the brains, and Denise here got the excellent people skills."

Denise shot Camilla a dirty look.

"If you must know, we met around two months ago," Camilla said.

"That's awfully fast, don't you think?" Denise's eyes never left Lindsey's face.

"You know what they say about lesbian relationships. Well, I suppose you wouldn't."

"So, you were together for a couple of weeks before you decided to move in?" Denise held her hand up, palm out, in Camilla's direction. "Don't answer for her. I'm sure she's capable of saying more than a few words."

Lindsey swallowed. "Well, I needed a place to stay, so Camilla invited me. It's just for a few months."

"How generous of you, Millie."

Camilla corrected her again. "It's Camilla."

"What is it that you do, Lindsey?" Denise asked.

"Well, I used to work at a call center selling insurance until recently. It isn't what I wanted to do with my life, but I needed a job after college, so I took it."

Camilla squeezed Lindsey's hand. "She's an artist, actually."

"Oh?" Denise gave Lindsey an icy look. "So you spend your days drawing pictures while leeching off my family's money?"

"For starters, it's my money, and I'll do what I want with it," Camilla said. "And Lindsey isn't leeching off anyone. Even if she was, it wouldn't justify how rude you're being."

"I'm just telling the truth, Millie. Can't you see that-"

"That's enough," Camilla said sharply. "If you say one more nasty thing about Lindsey, you can find somewhere else to stay tonight."

"It's my house too. You can't kick me out."

"Last time I checked, our parents left the house to me. And for a good reason."

Denise scoffed. "Because you're the fucking golden child."

"No, it's because I know the meaning of family," Camilla said. "But that doesn't mean I'm above kicking you out if you continue to disrespect Lindsey. So shut up and eat this lovely dinner that has been prepared for us."

Denise scowled, but she didn't say anything. She simply picked up her fork and continued to eat.

The rest of the meal passed in near silence, but the expression on Denise's face spoke volumes. She didn't like that Lindsey was here.

And she didn't like Lindsey.

After sitting through the whole meal, from appetizers to dessert, Camilla turned to Lindsey and gave her a strained smile.

"Darling, my sister and I have a lot to catch up on," she said. "We'll be in the drawing room if you need me."

"Yes, Mis-" Lindsey flushed. "Sure."

Lindsey kissed Camilla on the cheek and got out of there as fast as she could.

Lindsey was lying on the bed in her room with her headphones on, listening to music and messaging Faith, when Denise appeared at the foot of her bed.

Lindsey sat up with a start. "Denise. I didn't hear you come in." She hadn't even knocked, which had to be intentional.

"I just knew Camilla would put you in here." Denise glared around the room. "Typical. This was always the nicest of the guest suites. Only the most important visitors were allowed to stay here. Never our friends or relatives. Certainly not stragglers off the streets."

Lindsey sat up and watched Denise stroll around the room, examining everything. The woman walked over to the closet and opened the door. She pulled out a dress, the emerald one that Lindsey had worn that first night out in the garden.

"I suppose my sister bought all this for you?" Denise asked. "Either that, or selling insurance is more lucrative than I thought."

"Camilla did buy that for me." Lindsey crossed her arms. "So what if she did?"

"I'm not surprised. My sister always had such gaudy tastes."

Lindsey fumed. She'd had it with this woman. "What do you want?"

Denise stuck the dress back into the closet and shut the door. "Do you know what they used to call a woman like you? A woman who lives off the riches of a wealthy lover in exchange for providing certain other... benefits?" She returned to stand at the foot of Lindsey's bed. "A kept woman. It's more polite than 'gold-digger' I suppose. Or something even more unpleasant."

It wasn't hard for Lindsey to figure out what Denise meant. "I'm not after Camilla's money."

Denise scoffed. "Someone young and pretty like you? There's no reason for you to be with Millie otherwise."

"Did it ever occur to you that I like her? That I'm attracted to her? That I want to be with her?"

"Would you still want to be with her if it wasn't for her money?"

"Yes," Lindsey said.

"I don't believe you."

"It's a good thing that your opinion doesn't matter to me or Camilla one bit."

Denise gave a derisive chuckle. "You've got more bite than I expected. Is that how you managed to fool my sister? You manipulated her into thinking you actually like her?"

"I'm not manipulating her," Lindsey said. "Do you really think anyone could manipulate Camilla?"

"Well, you've obviously done something. It's clear that she's fallen hard for you."

"Did you just come in here to make snide remarks about me?"

"No. I came to tell you to stop screwing around with my sister."

Lindsey's brows drew together. Could it be that Denise was actually worried about Camilla, and not the family money? "Look, I'm not screwing around with Camilla. I'm not after her money. Our relationship has only just started, but I'm serious about her. Really."

"All right," Denise said. "Let's pretend for a minute that I believe you. You've known each other for a couple of months. You've been living together, here, for most of that time. Right now, you like her. But what's going to happen when the shine rubs off? You know what she's like, don't you? Temperamental, moody, controlling? You know what living with her is like?"

"Yes, but-"

"And you know about her illness, right? About how she can barely live a normal life?"

"That's not true. Her life is still a normal one. And it's

not a problem for me." Sure, Camilla had had a few flare-ups in the time Lindsey had been living with her. But Camilla managed just fine.

"You say that now, but you might not feel that way in a few months' time. She's what, 20 years older than you?"

"I'm 23," Lindsey said. Not that Denise cared about the details.

"You're still so young. What's going to happen when you decide that things are too hard? When you decide that no amount of money is worth being locked away in this manor with an emotionally stunted old woman?"

"That's-"

"Because it will happen. And Millie will be crushed."

"That's not going to happen!"

Denise stared at her, her eyes boring into Lindsey's. She shifted uncomfortably on the bed but didn't look away.

"Christ," Denise said. "You really believe that, don't you?"

"I do," Lindsey replied.

Denise shook her head. "Here I thought you were a gold-digger. But you're just naive. It's no wonder. You're barely more than a child."

"Maybe you're right. Maybe I am naive. Maybe I'll wake up one day and realize that I don't want this life with Camilla anymore." Lindsey clenched her fists in her lap. "I don't know what's going to happen in the future. But I know what I feel right now. And I care about Camilla more than I even know how to express. I'm not going to leave her. There's nowhere in the world I'd rather be than by her side."

"You're making a mistake," Denise said.

"Why are you trying so hard to turn me against Camilla?"

"I'm just trying to protect her."

"She doesn't need your protection," Lindsey said. "What she needs is your love and support, yet here you are, tearing her down behind her back. Some sister you are."

"You know nothing about this family. Don't talk about us like you do."

"I know enough. And you've shown me exactly who you are just now." Lindsey tried as hard as she could to channel Camilla's commanding manner. "Get out of my room."

To Lindsey's surprise, Denise turned her nose up and walked to the door.

Before Denise left the room, she addressed Lindsey. "Whatever happens, don't you dare hurt my sister." She slammed the door shut behind her.

Lindsey blew out a breath and collapsed onto the bed. As she lay there with her eyes closed, she recalled something Denise had said earlier.

It's clear that she's fallen hard for you.

Camilla? Falling for me? Lindsey doubted that. It was all just part of the lie.

But as Lindsey lay there, she realized something. Everything she'd said to Denise about her feelings for Camilla?

Not a single word of it had been a lie.

CHAPTER SEVENTEEN

For the days that followed, Lindsey avoided Denise. She couldn't be in the woman's presence without feeling enraged. Denise probably didn't even notice that Lindsey was avoiding her. On the rare occasion that they crossed paths, Denise appeared determined to ignore Lindsey's existence completely, which Lindsey didn't mind one bit.

She hadn't told Camilla about Denise's visit to her room. Between work and her sister's visit, Camilla was stressed out enough. Nevertheless, she insisted that they all have meals together. These were always awkward affairs.

Breakfast that morning was no exception.

"Denise," Camilla began. "The disaster relief foundation the company supports is holding a charity auction. How about we go through some of mother's jewelry and select a few pieces to donate?"

"Just do it without me," Denise said. "I have too much to do."

"Let me guess. Work?"

That was something Camilla and Denise had in common. Lindsey didn't know why Denise even came to visit considering how much time she spent locked in her room working.

"Well, not all of us can just lie around all day." Denise looked pointedly at Lindsey. "Some of us have jobs."

Lindsey returned Denise's glare.

Camilla put down her knife and fork carefully. "Denise, didn't I tell you to stop being rude to Lindsey?"

"Oh, stop acting like she's some innocent little girl," Denise said. "Lindsey here can dish it out just as well as she can take it."

"What's that supposed to mean?" Camilla's eyes flicked between Denise and Lindsey. "What's going on?"

Lindsey said nothing. After all, she wasn't the one who had started this.

"Denise? You said something to her, didn't you?"

"I don't know what you're talking about," Denise said. "I didn't say anything."

"For a politician, you're not very good at lying."

"Fine. I didn't say anything that wasn't true."

Camilla's eyes clouded over. "You *bitch*. What the hell did you say to her?"

"I'm just looking out for you, Millie."

"Oh, because you've done so much of that in the past, haven't you?"

Lindsey tried as hard as she could to dissolve into her chair. Luckily, June chose that moment to reenter the room, carrying a pot of coffee, which she placed on the table before Camilla. It seemed to remind Camilla that Lindsey was still sitting there.

"Lindsey, darling," Camilla said through gritted teeth. "Do you mind? I need to talk to my sister. Alone."

"Okay." Lindsey got up and followed June out into the hall.

Seconds later, the dining room erupted into shouts.

"I can't believe you said that!" Camilla yelled.

Lindsey stopped just within earshot.

"I'm trying to keep you from getting hurt," Denise replied.

"That's bullshit. You don't get to disappear from my life for months, even years at a time, then come back and stick your nose in my business and pretend to care.

"I'm not pretending, Millie. I do care."

"You have some way of showing it. Calling Lindsey a gold-digger? Trying to drive the person I care about the most away?"

June cleared her throat. "I would have thought you'd learned your lesson about listening at doors."

Lindsey jumped. She hadn't realized that June was still there. "Er, right."

"Trust me. You don't want to get caught up in one of their fights. It's best to just let them talk it out."

"So, they're always like this?" Lindsey asked.

"Their relationship is… complicated." June said. "Now, you didn't get to finish your breakfast. If you'd like, I can bring you something."

"No, it's fine."

"All right." June stood in place, waiting for Lindsey to leave.

"I'll just go then."

June nodded. As Lindsey walked away, she could feel June's eyes on her.

Lindsey spent the morning outside, attempting to sketch the wild, overgrown orchard at the back of the estate. It was no coincidence that it was as far from the manor as possible. The tension between Camilla and Denise seemed to permeate the entire house.

But when Lindsey went back to the manor for lunch, both Camilla and Denise were nowhere to be found. The house felt eerily empty, and there was no one else in the dining room. When Lindsey asked June where Camilla was, the housekeeper informed her that both sisters had requested lunch in their rooms. That was unusual. Camilla never took her meals anywhere but the dining room unless she wasn't feeling well.

Lindsey ate lunch alone, then headed to her room, debating with herself about whether she should go to Camilla, or give her some space. She was so lost in thought that she almost didn't see Denise standing by the entrance to her rooms.

Lindsey stopped in her tracks. "What are you doing here?"

"Can we talk?" Denise asked.

"Sure." When Denise didn't move, Lindsey realized that she was waiting to be invited in. "Come in."

They entered Lindsey's sitting room. Lindsey sat down on the lounge, and Denise took a seat in the Victorian armchair next to the far window. Lindsey crossed her arms and waited. If Denise wanted to insult her again, she wasn't just going to sit there and take it.

"I'm-" Denise cleared her throat. "I'm sorry."

Lindsey said nothing. Denise was going to have to do better than that.

"I'm sorry for all the things I said about you. That you're a gold-digger, and after Camilla's money. It was rude and hurtful, and I apologize."

"Did Camilla tell you to apologize to me?" Lindsey asked.

Denise looked down at her shoes. "Yes. But I really do mean it. I was cruel to you. You deserve an apology."

"What about Camilla?"

"What do you mean?"

"I wasn't the only one you said nasty things about. What about everything you said about her?"

Denise examined Lindsey. "You really do care about her, don't you? Yes, I'm sorry for all the things I said about Millie —I mean, Camilla—too. I didn't mean them. I was just trying to drive you away, to protect her. And I do love her, even though she prefers to think otherwise."

"It sounds like she has good reasons for feeling that way."

"You're right. I know I haven't always been the best sister. Actually, I was a terrible sister from the start. After me, our mother was told she wouldn't be able to have any more children. Ten years later, a happy accident named Camilla was born. Here I was, an only child who was used to having all my parents' attention, and suddenly, this little miracle baby was the center of their world. Our parents spoiled Camilla to pieces. I was jealous of her, so I treated her badly. Naturally, she started to lash out at me too, and we've been trapped in this cycle of resentment ever since.

"Then, after both our parents passed, I found it too painful to be in this house, so I stopped coming to see

Camilla, and she's never forgiven me." Denise leaned forward and put her elbows on her knees. "For the past few years, I've been trying to make amends. But Camilla has a habit of holding onto old hurts. And no matter what I do, she just can't let go of the image of me she's built up over time."

Lindsey felt a pang of sympathy. Denise was no angel, but Camilla wasn't innocent in all this. Camilla had been attacking her sister with snide comments from the moment Denise had arrived at the manor.

"What has she told you about me?" Denise asked.

"She said you've never approved of the life she lives."

Denise sighed. "Let me guess. She told you that she had to come out to me three times before I believed her?"

Lindsey nodded.

"She's never going to let go of that. It's true. But this was more than 20 years ago. It was still the nineties. People weren't as accepting back then. I came around eventually."

What do you want, a medal? Lindsey thought. But she kept her mouth shut.

"And when I did come around, I fully supported her. Like when she had her first girlfriend. Camilla must have been 17." A faint smile crossed Denise's face. "She had the gall to bring this girlfriend of hers to a party here at the manor as her date. It wasn't just any party, mind you. It was a high-society party, and one of the first of the season.

"It caused a huge scandal. Well, it would have, if I hadn't put a stop to all the gossip. The moment Camilla and her date walked in, this group of girls started saying the meanest things about them. Camilla didn't hear any of it, but I did. I had the whole lot of them very publicly kicked out, made it clear that they weren't welcome here ever again, and I made sure everyone knew exactly why. I spent the next few weeks defending Camilla and her girlfriend, telling off anyone who dared say a bad word about them. It took a while, but eventually, everyone accepted them."

"Did Camilla know all this was going on?" Lindsey asked.

"Of course not," Denise said. "I made sure she was kept in the dark. She's my baby sister, after all. I wanted to protect her from all the cruelty out there in the world."

"Maybe if you told her, she'd realize that you cared about her all along."

"It wouldn't help," Denise said. "The thing about Camilla is that she's so determined not to rely on other people that she pushes everyone away. She's always been like that, ever since we were kids. And everything she's gone through with her health has made her even more cynical and blind to all the people out there who love and care about her. Perhaps it makes it easier for her to justify her decision to never let anyone in."

It was true that Camilla valued her independence. And Lindsey remembered Camilla's surprise when she realized how worried Lindsey had been after she'd sneaked into Camilla's rooms that night so long ago. It hadn't even occurred to Camilla that Lindsey cared about what was going on with her.

"The problem is, on the rare occasion Camilla lets someone in, she falls hard and fast," Denise continued. "I mean, look at the two of you. It hasn't even been two months, and it's clear that she's already crazy about you.

The flip-side of that is that when things don't work out, she takes it hard. If you break her heart, it will crush her."

Lindsey, break Camilla's heart? "Honestly, I think you're overestimating how serious things are between the two of us," she said. "I don't think I could break her heart."

Denise stared at Lindsey, shaking her head. "You don't even know what you have, do you?"

There was a knock on the door.

"That's my cue to leave." Denise got up and opened the door. Camilla was standing in the doorway. "She's all yours, Camilla." Denise gave Lindsey a polite nod, before slipping away.

Camilla sat down on the lounge next to Lindsey and placed a hand on her thigh. "So, was my sister's apology satisfactory?"

Lindsey nodded. "She seemed sincere."

"I'm glad you think so. She's never been good at apologizing. After everything she said to you, I should have just kicked her out of the house."

"It's okay," Lindsey said. "I think she meant well. She was trying to protect you in her own way."

"The only thing she was trying to protect is the family fortune."

"That's not true. She was worried that I'd break your heart."

"Really?" Camilla looked out the window pensively. "Huh. It looks like we played our roles a little too well."

Lindsey felt a sinking in her stomach. *Right. This is all just pretend.* "Yeah. I guess we did."

CHAPTER EIGHTEEN

Camilla slipped into the bed next to Lindsey and pulled the silk sheets up to cover them both. "Thanks again for agreeing to this charade."

"I don't mind," Lindsey replied. "It's been kind of fun."

Lindsey peered at her Mistress, searching her face. Could Camilla detect the longing in Lindsey's voice? Could she hear the real meaning behind Lindsey's words? Could she tell that for Lindsey, this wasn't a charade at all?

But Camilla's mind was elsewhere. "I'm just glad Denise is leaving in the morning," she said. "She's been getting on my nerves all week. She's so overbearing and controlling. And I'm going to strangle her if she calls me Millie one more time. She knows how much I hate that childish nickname."

After Denise's apology, the tension between Camilla and Denise had settled. But that hadn't stopped the two of them from fighting like teenage sisters. Lindsey bit back a smile. Camilla was such a contradiction of a woman. Sometimes warm, sometimes prickly. Sometimes she seemed older than her years. Other times she was liable to throw tantrums and indulge in sweet things like a spoiled princess.

"Is something funny?" Camilla asked.

"No, Mistress," Lindsey replied. "Not at all."

"Maybe I'm overreacting. It's just that, Denise frustrates me sometimes." Camilla folded her hands behind her head and looked up at the ceiling. "But she's the only family I have left. My parents were older when they had me, and they passed away when I was still in my early twenties, but by that time, Denise was already busy with her own family and her career. She didn't have time for me. I began to resent her for it, and we grew distant. I sometimes wish we were closer, but she doesn't want that."

"Maybe she does, but she's not good at showing it," Lindsey said. "She did come here to visit you, after all. You should give her a chance."

Camilla raised an eyebrow.

"Er, it's just a suggestion, Mistress."

"Perhaps you're right." Camilla paused. "I was thinking of inviting her family to come stay for the holidays, but I changed my mind after all the drama of this week. Maybe I should reconsider."

"I think she'd like that."

Camilla leaned back and stared at Lindsey. "What did the two of you talk about?"

"Nothing much," Lindsey said hurriedly.

"It doesn't matter. Once again, we're talking about my sister when we could be doing more exciting things." Beneath the sheets, Camilla's hand crept up Lindsey's thigh, pushing up the hem of her nightie.

Lindsey gave Camilla her most innocent look. "Like what, Mistress?"

Camilla moved in closer and drew her lips up the side of Lindsey's neck, all the way to her ear. "Like your Mistress finally letting you pleasure her."

"Do you mean-" Lindsey's words died in her chest as Camilla kissed her way down the side of Lindsey's throat.

"Yes," Camilla said. "But you first."

Camilla took hold of the hem of Lindsey's nightie and tugged it up over her head. She wasn't wearing anything underneath. Camilla swept her lips down to Lindsey's nipples. They were already hard from just the suggestion of getting to pleasure her Mistress.

"I'm going to need to get warmed up." Camilla pushed Lindsey's shoulders down onto the bed. "And nothing gets me hotter than wringing one of those delicious orgasms from you."

Lindsey stared shamelessly at Camilla above her. Her silk nightgown was so thin it might as well have been invisible. Just weeks ago, Lindsey had been adamant that she wasn't attracted to Camilla because she had 'the wrong equipment.' Now, every part of Camilla's body made Lindsey throb. Her supple curves. Her soft, insistent lips. The tiny pebbled nipples poking through the fabric of her nightgown.

Camilla slid her free hand down to where Lindsey's thighs met and teased her swelling clit. Lindsey drew in a gasping breath. Camilla leaned down and sucked Lindsey's nipple through her teeth, eliciting a strangled whimper. She tweaked the other nipple with her fingers.

"Oh, Mistress. That feels so good." Lindsey writhed on

the bed, twisting the sheets around her. She had never gone from zero to wet and panting so quickly. Her gasps turned to moans as Camilla increased the pace.

"Do you want your Mistress to fuck you?" Camilla asked.

"Yes," Lindsey replied. "Please!"

Camilla glided her fingers down Lindsey's slit and entered her carefully. Lindsey quivered. She had no idea how many fingers were inside her, but they were enough to fill her up. Camilla began to delve in and out, first slowly, then hard and fast.

Lindsey arched up, pushing back into Camilla's hand. She reached up to grab onto Camilla's hip, but all she could grasp was a fistful of silk. She clung onto it tightly. This was so different from when Camilla had fucked her with a strap-on. This way, Camilla had far more control. And with her fingers inside stroking Lindsey's sweet spot, and her thumb grazing Lindsey's bud, she was being flooded with pleasure from all angles.

"Mistress!" She arched up one final time and threw her head back as waves of ecstasy washed over her. Lindsey held on to Camilla until her tremors subsided and she fell back to the bed.

That earth-shattering orgasm should have left Lindsey spent. Instead, it made her even more eager to please her Mistress.

"Thank you, Mistress," she said. "Can I serve you now?"

"Yes." Camilla's voice rang with passion. "Just remember what I said. I like to hold the reins."

Camilla threw one leg over Lindsey, straddling her, and pulled her silk nightgown up her hips. The lips between her thighs had a wet sheen, like dew on a flower. It wasn't like Lindsey had never seen a pussy before. But she had never seen one that made her want to touch it, and taste it, and explore it. Not until now.

Camilla shuffled up the bed, holding her nightie around her waist, until she was kneeling over Lindsey's head. "Do you want to taste me?"

Lindsey's breath shuddered. "Yes, Mistress." Camilla's intentions were clear. 'Holding the reins' wasn't just a metaphor.

Camilla grabbed onto the headboard. Gently, she lowered herself down onto Lindsey's mouth. Lindsey slipped her tongue into Camilla slit, lapping at her folds. They were like liquid silk, and so hot that they seemed to burn. She slid her tongue down to Camilla's entrance, darting it inside. Her upper lip tickled Camilla's clit.

"God, yes." Camilla shifted her hips, pressing herself against Lindsey's lips.

Lindsey got the message loud and clear. She took Camilla in her mouth, licking and sucking her swollen nub. Camilla gyrated her hips, riding against Lindsey's face. The silk of Camilla's nightie fell down around Lindsey's head, Camilla's dizzying scent enveloping her.

"Faster," Camilla urged.

Lindsey redoubled her efforts, devouring her Mistress. Atop her, Camilla moaned and bucked, nearly smothering Lindsey with her thrusts. The bed rocked and creaked around them.

Finally, a cry erupted from Camilla's chest, and her thighs began to shake. Lindsey licked away gently, until

Camilla rose up, climbing off Lindsey and collapsing next to her.

Lindsey rolled onto her side and ran her palm up Camilla's chest. "How did I do, Mistress?"

"I think you know the answer to that." Suddenly, Camilla slapped her hand to her forehead. "Oh, christ."

"What's the matter?"

"I got caught up in the moment. I forgot that you've never done that before."

Lindsey frowned. "Did I do something wrong?"

"Lindsey, if you did something wrong, I wouldn't be lying here completely unable to move."

"What is it, then?"

"It's just that, this was your first experience pleasuring a woman," Camilla said. "And it involved me sitting on your face."

Lindsey burst out laughing. "That's what you're worried about? It's not a bad thing. As far as first experiences go, it's one that I'll never forget."

"Wouldn't you have preferred something more intimate?"

Lindsey shrugged. "That felt intimate to me. Everything we do does. What's more intimate than submission?"

A soft smile formed on Camilla's lips. "I feel the same way. We really get each other, don't we?"

It was true. Lindsey had never been with anyone who understood her desires like Camilla did. But it was so much more than that. More than just Mistress and submissive, more than two people with an arrangement.

There was no denying it. Lindsey had fallen for Camilla so deeply. She hadn't forgotten that this was supposed to be pretend. But it felt more real than anything she'd ever experienced.

Lindsey looked at Camilla. "Mistress?"

"Yes?" Camilla said.

"I'm glad I get to share all these firsts with you."

"So am I." Camilla rolled onto her stomach and gathered her hair over one shoulder. "And I've enjoyed having you sleep next to me these past few days. How do you feel about sleeping in my bedroom from now on?"

"I'd like that," Lindsey said.

"And you can come into my rooms whenever you like. Just don't mess anything up."

"Yes, Mistress."

Camilla lay back down and drew Lindsey's head to rest on her shoulder. "By the way, I was going to reschedule that dinner party for next Saturday, but a friend of mine is having a last-minute engagement party. How would you like to come with me to that instead?"

"Sure," Lindsey murmured. "I'd love to."

"You're going to have a great time. Vanessa really knows how to throw a party."

CHAPTER NINETEEN

Camilla knocked on the door to the penthouse apartment. Lindsey could hear the faint sounds of music and chatter inside. She glanced at Camilla. There was a question Lindsey had wanted to ask her Mistress ever since Camilla invited her to this party. It shouldn't have been a difficult question to ask. Nevertheless, it filled Lindsey's stomach with butterflies.

"Mistress?" Lindsey asked.

"Yes?" Camilla said.

"If people ask about the two of us, what should I tell them?"

"What do you want to tell them?"

"That I'm your girlfriend? It would be simpler after all."

"After a week of playing my girlfriend for Denise, you're not tired of it?"

"Not at all."

Even after Denise left, Lindsey and Camilla had continued with their feigned intimacy. It was almost as though they hoped that if they pretended hard enough, the lie would become real. At least, that was how Lindsey felt. But surely Camilla had noticed that this was no longer an act for Lindsey. Surely Camilla could tell that Lindsey's feelings were real.

Surely Camilla felt it too.

"Okay then. You're my girlfriend." The corners of Camilla's lips curled up. "And once again, I give you permission to not call me Mistress."

Lindsey smiled. It was impossible not to react to Camilla's smile, and her bright eyes, and that stern but playful tone of hers that sent pleasant shivers through Lindsey's entire body.

The door swung open, and a raven-haired woman with pale skin appeared. "Camilla," the woman said. "So glad you could make it." She pulled Camilla into an embrace.

"I wouldn't miss this," Camilla replied. "Congratulations on the engagement."

"Thank you." The woman broke off and turned to Lindsey. "And you must be Lindsey. My name's Vanessa. It's lovely to meet you."

Lindsey stumbled over a greeting. Her stomach swam with both nerves and excitement.

"Here, I brought you a small engagement present." Camilla handed Vanessa a bottle of whiskey with a yellowing label and a bow tied around its neck.

Vanessa took the bottle and held it up to the light. Her mouth dropped open. "Where on earth did you find this? Last I heard, there were only fifty bottles left in the world."

"I convinced an old family friend to part with it as part of a business deal."

"This is incredible, Camilla. Thank you."

Lindsey and Camilla followed Vanessa inside. The enormous, lavishly decorated apartment held a few dozen people, all dressed to the nines. Lindsey now understood why Camilla had bought her a new dress for the occasion.

"I have a gift for Mel too," Camilla said. "I made a donation to the legal aid clinic where she works. I thought she'd like that more than something material."

"Melanie will be thrilled." Vanessa looked around. "She's here somewhere. I'm going to go find her. Make yourselves at home."

Camilla led Lindsey over to a small home bar to the side. They helped themselves to some wine.

Camilla spoke to Lindsey under her breath. "Don't tell anyone this, but Vanessa owns a string of BDSM clubs around the country. There's one right here in the city. Lilith's Den."

"Really?" Lindsey looked over at the woman, who was chatting at the other side of the room. "Is that how you know each other?"

"Yes. I did some business with her when her company was just starting out. It must have been ten years ago. But we didn't really get to know each other until we crossed paths at Lilith's Den a few months later. I'll take you there sometime if you'd like."

"I'd love that, Mistress," Lindsey said. There was no one close enough to overhear them.

"Actually, that's how a lot of us know each other." Camilla looked around the room. "Half the guests here go to that club."

"Really? But everyone seems so proper."

"Unlike the two of us, who look like a pair of sexual deviants?"

"That's a good point."

"You should see this crowd at Lilith's Den." Camilla leaned in and spoke quietly. "Between you and me, it's always the proper ones who are the most perverted. There's nothing quite like sitting through a business meeting with a woman you saw the night before getting spanked on a stage in nothing but a corset and a thong."

Heat crept up Lindsey's face. She wasn't sure if it was embarrassment or arousal.

As the two of them mingled, Lindsey found herself distracted by the idea that some of the people she met were secretly like her and Camilla. She couldn't help but try to pick them out. Of the couples, she thought she saw a few signs. They would give it away with a possessive touch, or a deferential look, or a disguised piece of jewelry that would have been impossible to spot unless she knew what to look for.

Camilla led her over to a group of women lounging nearby. Vanessa was there, perched on the arm of a chair. Below her sat a woman with a serious face who looked around Lindsey's age. She had to be Vanessa's fiancée.

"Camilla," the woman said. "Vanessa told me about your gift. Thanks, that's so thoughtful of you."

"It's my pleasure, Mel," Camilla replied.

She and Lindsey sat down, and Camilla introduced Lindsey to Mel, as well as the others who were sitting across from them. There was a slender woman with short blonde hair and a fitted suit, who had her arm slung casually around the shoulders of a tiny brunette. Everyone seemed to know each other well.

"So, who's going to be your maid of honor, Vanessa?" The blonde woman asked. Vicki was her name. "I can throw you an amazing bachelorette party."

Camilla scoffed. "Sure, if you want strippers and booze, go with Vicki. If you decide you want something more sophisticated, I'll be right here."

Vicki shot Camilla a look. "There are sophisticated strippers. I can put you in touch with some if you like, Camilla. Maybe it'll help with that stick up your-"

"Ladies, please," Vanessa said. "We haven't thought that far ahead yet. Besides, we might not even have bridesmaids. We're thinking of doing something small."

"Vanessa, passing up a chance to make an ostentatious display of love?" Camilla said. "I'll believe it when I see it. Which reminds me, what was the proposal like?"

"If you must know, I took Melanie to a cozy little cabin and proposed to her there." Vanessa's hand fell to Mel's shoulder. "It was all very low key."

"Low key?" Mel said. "The 'cozy little cabin' was two stories high and at the top of a mountain. We had to take a helicopter to get there. And there were fireworks, and-"

"Like I said, low key." Vanessa squeezed Mel's shoulder. "She won't let me spoil her anywhere near as much as I want to."

"That's because you always go overboard." Mel looked at the others. "She wants to have the wedding on a private island. Can you believe it?"

"I'm open to other ideas," Vanessa said. "I recently

purchased a lovely villa in the French countryside. It would make the perfect wedding venue."

"What's wrong with having the wedding here in the city?"

"I suppose that would make things easier. And that way, we could invite even more people, and make the whole thing bigger."

Mel twisted the ring around her finger, her face frozen in alarm. Vanessa seemed completely oblivious. Mel looked like she was about to protest when Vanessa spotted someone by the door.

"More guests," she said. "Let's go say hello."

The two women wandered off, leaving Camilla and Lindsey with Vicki and the brunette, April. Camilla had told Lindsey that April and Vicki were a couple, but Lindsey could sense a heavy tension hanging between them.

April nudged Vicki with her elbow. "What was that you were saying about putting Camilla in touch with some strippers?"

"I was kidding," Vicki said. "I don't know any strippers. At least, not anymore."

"Anymore? What does that mean?"

Vicki shrugged. "It's no secret the kind of life I lived before we met. But it's all behind me now." She crossed her legs. "Do you have something against strippers? How narrow-minded of you. Stripping is a legitimate profession like any other."

April folded her arms across her chest. "That's not what I meant, and you know it."

"Honestly, I had no idea you were so judgmental."

"Stop trying to turn this around on me, Victoria."

Camilla tapped Lindsey's arm and spoke into her ear. "Let's leave those two alone."

Camilla and Lindsey wandered off toward a table of canapes. Lindsey was just relieved to get away from the quarreling couple.

"Don't let those two fool you," Camilla said. "They're always arguing about something or other. I think they enjoy it. Give it five minutes, and they'll be making out in a dark closet somewhere."

An hour passed, and another, and Lindsey began to loosen up. The drinks helped. So did talking to the other guests. Although half of them seemed as accustomed to the glitz and glamour around them as Camilla did, the other half seemed just as dazzled by their surroundings as Lindsey was.

And being here, playing Camilla's girlfriend for all the world to see, was making it all the more apparent that Lindsey wanted everything between them to be real. She didn't know what to do with all these feelings. She'd never felt like this about anyone before.

Did Camilla feel it too? She'd brought Lindsey here tonight as her date. But what if this was just Camilla showing Lindsey off to her friends? Didn't most men do this with their sugar babies? Dress them up like dolls and show them off as status symbols?

Camilla placed a hand on Lindsey's arm. "I need to speak with April. I'll be right back."

"Okay." Lindsey's voice came out as a nervous squeak, but Camilla didn't seem to notice.

As Camilla disappeared into the crowd, Lindsey took another sip of her wine. Her eyes were drawn to Vanessa and Mel, who were standing to the side, arms around each other, smiling. Over the course of the night, she'd heard snippets of the story of Mel and Vanessa's relationship. It was the kind of romance that Lindsey used to fantasize about. Being swept off her feet by some mysterious lover. In Lindsey's fantasies, that lover had always been a man. Of course, that had all changed.

Lindsey finished off the last of her wine and went over to the bar. She refilled her glass and drank some more. How was she supposed to continue everything with Camilla as they had before, knowing what she now felt? How was she supposed to go on?

Her thoughts were interrupted when someone sidled up beside her. It was Vicki. The blonde woman poured two glasses of wine, then turned to Lindsey, a knowing look in her eyes.

"So." Vicki picked up one of the glasses and took a long sip, studying Lindsey carefully. "You're this mysterious guest of Camilla's."

Lindsey nodded. "Yep." She wasn't in the mood to elaborate. And she was tired of lying.

"How long have the two of you been together?"

"A couple of months, I guess," Lindsey mumbled.

Vicki put down her glass and held up her hands apologetically. "Sorry, I didn't mean to pry. Sticking my nose in people's business is a bad habit of mine."

"It's okay. It's not you, it's me."

An uncomfortable silence hung in the air.

"Is something the matter between the two of you?" Vicki asked.

Lindsey hesitated. Vicki seemed to think that Camilla

and Lindsey's relationship was real. She was one of Camilla's close friends. Didn't she know the truth?

"What has Camilla told you about me?" Lindsey asked.

"She hasn't said much. Just that you've been living with her. I didn't even realize you were a couple until tonight." Vicki grimaced. "There I go again, running my mouth. I didn't mean anything by it. It's just that Camilla doesn't talk about relationships much."

"No, once again, it isn't you." Lindsey didn't know why she was saying this. "We're not really a couple."

"You're not?"

"I'm her sugar baby."

"Oh."

An awkward silence followed.

"And that bothers you?" Vicki asked.

"Yes," Lindsey replied.

"Because you have feelings for her?"

Lindsey nodded.

"Then you should tell her."

"I can't. I have no idea if she feels the same way."

"There's only one way to find out," Vicki said.

Lindsey just sighed.

The conversation lapsed into silence again. Vicki crossed her arms and looked out into the crowd. Lindsey sipped at her wine. Her eyes fell on Camilla, who was at the other end of the room, talking to April.

Suddenly, Vicki spoke. "It's terrifying, isn't it?"

"What?" Lindsey said.

"Love."

Lindsey looked at Vicki. The blonde woman was staring in the same direction Lindsey had been looking.

But Vicki was looking at April, her eyes filled with passion.

"It's this incredible, impossible, overwhelming thing that drives you crazy, and upends your whole existence," Vicki said. "It makes you wonder how a single person can cause so much turmoil."

Was that what this feeling was? Love?

"But it's worth it. Even if it means putting your heart on the line and risking everything, it's so worth it." Vicki turned to Lindsey. "Tell her. Before it's too late. You'll regret it otherwise."

Lindsey's pulse quickened. Across the room, Camilla and April were working their way over to where Lindsey and Vicki stood. Lindsey's eyes met Camilla's. Camilla gave her that warm smile that always made her heart melt.

"You're right," Lindsey said softly. "I have to tell her."

Moments later, Camilla and April joined the two of them by the bar. Vicki picked up the two glasses of wine and handed one to April, who thanked her with a kiss. It was clear that there was only love there. Apparently, their argument earlier had meant nothing.

Camilla slipped an arm around Lindsey's waist. "I hope you weren't causing any trouble, Vicki." The tone of her voice suggested she was only half joking.

"Don't worry," Vicki said. "My troublemaking days are over. Now, I only meddle for good reasons." She took her girlfriend's arm and tipped her head toward Lindsey. "I'll see you later."

As the two of them walked away, Vicki mouthed the words "tell her" to Lindsey behind Camilla's back.

"Well, that was odd." Camilla reached out and brushed Lindsey's hair out of her face. "Are you having a nice time?"

"Yeah," Lindsey said. "I am."

Camilla examined Lindsey's face. "Are you all right, darling?"

"Yeah. I drank a little too much, that's all." She'd only had a few glasses of wine, but right now, Lindsey felt like her world had been tipped on its axis.

"Oh?" Camilla took her hand. "Do you need some water? Or do you want to go lie down? There's a spare room just down the hall."

"No, I'm fine."

"Well, it's getting late anyway. Should we head home?"

"Home sounds great," Lindsey replied.

As she and Camilla said their goodbyes, Lindsey realized that for the first time, she'd called the manor home.

They spent the car ride back to the manor in near silence. Camilla seemed to accept that Lindsey had drunk too much. But that was just another excuse. As the wine wore off, Lindsey was left with a churning in her stomach that had nothing to do with being drunk.

As soon as they pulled up outside the manor, Lindsey practically ran inside. She knew she had to tell Camilla how she felt. Why was this so hard? When did she become so anxious and fearful? The old Lindsey would have shouted her feelings from a mountaintop.

"Lindsey?" Camilla's footsteps echoed across the entrance hall. "Are you all right?"

Lindsey stopped by the stairs, her arms hugging herself in the cold. *I'm fine*, she tried to say. But she couldn't lie anymore. Her feelings toward Camilla were so strong that they hurt.

"Lindsey." Camilla took her hand and guided her to sit on the bottom step of the grand staircase. "What's going on?"

"Why did you take me to that party tonight?" It wasn't what Lindsey really wanted to say. But she needed some hint, some inkling that everything between them wasn't just a lie.

"Because I thought that you'd enjoy it," Camilla replied.

"So it wasn't so you could show your sugar baby off to your friends?"

"Of course not. Do you really think I'd do that?"

"No, I don't. But I wanted to be sure."

"Sure of what?" Camilla searched Lindsey's face. "What's going on?"

Lindsey's voice stuck in her throat. Her heart was pounding so hard, she felt like it would burst. She took a few deep breaths. Because of Camilla, Lindsey had faced her fears once already, that morning in her sunny studio. She could do it again.

"Camilla," Lindsey said. "I don't want this to be pretend anymore."

"What do you mean?"

"These past months, they've been some of the best of my life. It's all been like a dream."

Camilla patted Lindsey's hand. "I'm glad you've been enjoying life here at the manor."

"No, I mean… It's not because of this house, or the expensive clothes, or the gifts. It's because of you."

"Because of me?"

"Yes. Is that so hard to believe?" Lindsey stared at Camilla's bewildered face. Could it be that she really had no idea how Lindsey felt? That she was so determined to live her life alone that she couldn't see what was right in front of her?

"What are you saying?" Camilla asked.

"I'm saying that I'm in love with you."

"Oh." Camilla fell silent.

A lump formed in Lindsey's throat. She was wrong. She had read it all wrong. "Forget it. I never should have said anything."

"No, that's not… I'm sorry. I didn't know. I never thought-"

"Of course you didn't." Tears fell from Lindsey's eyes. "I'm just someone you're paying, like June. How could I be so stupi-"

"Lindsey, stop." Camilla reached out and cradled the side of Lindsey's face. "You're not just someone I'm paying. You're so much more to me. You always have been." Camilla brushed a tear from Lindsey's cheek with her thumb. "What I'm trying to say is, I never thought that you'd return my feelings."

Lindsey's heart skittered. "Return your feelings?"

"Oh, Lindsey. These past few months have been like something out of a dream for me too. And all because of you. I feel the same way you do."

"You do?"

"I do," Camilla said. "It's just that, I didn't plan for this to happen. I'm not good at dealing with anything unexpected."

"Really?" Lindsey blinked away the last of her tears. "I haven't noticed."

Smiling, Camilla pulled Lindsey in close. "I want this to be real too. From now on, no more pretending."

"Mistress, I stopped pretending weeks ago."

Camilla cupped Lindsey's face. Her lips met Lindsey's in a soft, steady kiss. Lindsey dissolved into her. Now that their feelings were finally out in the open, the kiss seemed so much sweeter.

But Lindsey was all too aware that not everything was out in the open. She'd told a little white lie the day they had met. And she still hadn't told Camilla the truth.

Lindsey pushed the thought aside. She didn't want to ruin this perfect moment.

CHAPTER TWENTY

"Lindsey?" Camilla called from the hall. "Where on earth are you?"

Lindsey cursed. She hadn't finished setting up yet. "I'm in the dining room."

Moments later, Camilla appeared in the doorway. She stared, first at Lindsey, who was standing next to the dining cart, then at the table where breakfast was laid out. "What's going on?"

"I'm serving you breakfast, Mistress," Lindsey replied.

Camilla looked at Lindsey, her eyes narrowed. "What have you done with June? The only thing that could keep her from her duties is being tied up in the basement."

"June's fine. She's in her room relaxing. I told her that I'd take care of breakfast this morning." It had taken a while to convince the housekeeper to let Lindsey take over, but she'd agreed in the end.

Camilla crossed her arms. "June's in on this too?"

Lindsey nodded.

"Really, both of you should know better. I don't like disruptions to my routine."

"I just want to serve you, Mistress." Lindsey bowed her head and peered up at Camilla. But her expression was inscrutable.

Camilla walked over to where Lindsey stood. She grabbed Lindsey's chin and tilted her head up. "You're lucky that I find this very sweet. I'll allow it. This time."

"Thank you, Mistress."

"Continue." Camilla took her seat at the head of the table. Lindsey had left Camilla a newspaper in its usual place beside her plate, but Camilla didn't pick it up. Instead, she sat back and watched Lindsey, her lips curved up slightly.

Lindsey continued setting everything up. "What do you have planned for today, Mistress?" She asked Camilla this question every day, even though her answer was always the same.

"I have some work to do in the morning," Camilla said. "But I'll be finished with everything by lunchtime. After that, I was thinking we could spend the afternoon in the playroom."

"The afternoon? What about your schedule?"

Camilla raised an eyebrow. "Are you questioning your Mistress?"

"No, Mistress," Lindsey said hurriedly. "I can't wait."

"Good. Because I have something special planned."

Lindsey's stomach flipped. She knew what that something special was. They'd talked about it already. And it excited her.

Lindsey placed the pot of coffee on the table in front of her Mistress. "All done. Your breakfast is served."

Camilla surveyed the spread laid out before her. She poured herself a cup of coffee, then helped herself to her usual dishes. Then she picked up her knife and fork and took a bite of her eggs, chewing slowly and deliberately.

Lindsey stood in place next to her Mistress, waiting for her approval. She'd been planning this for days. Even with June's instructions written down, it had taken her several tries to get everything exactly the way Camilla liked it.

Finally, Camilla placed her knife and fork down. "This is very good. But there's something missing." She beckoned Lindsey closer. "Something important."

Lindsey scanned the table before her. "What is it?" She was sure she'd thought of everything.

"You." Camilla grabbed Lindsey's arm and drew her onto her lap, planting a deep, possessive kiss on her lips. "Now put that cart away and join me at the table. Your Mistress commands it."

After lunch, Lindsey and Camilla had a long, sensual bath, before heading to the playroom. Both of them were wearing nothing but robes.

As Lindsey entered the room, her eyes were drawn to the foot of the bed. The drapes had been tied back carefully, leaving the X-shaped cross that was built into the frame completely exposed. That had to be deliberate.

Camilla led Lindsey to the table. Once again, the wooden chest with Camilla's initials on the lid sat on top of it. Camilla untied the belt of Lindsey's robe and slipped it from her shoulders, baring her naked body.

Camilla tapped the table next to the box. "Sit up here."

Lindsey took a seat on the edge of the table and watched her Mistress open the box, once again using the lid to hide its contents from view. First, Camilla pulled out the blue and gold wrist cuffs. Then, she took out a second pair of cuffs that were identical, but slightly bigger. They even had the same little gold tag with Camilla's initials on them. Finally, she pulled a blindfold out of the chest and set it down on the table next to the four pairs of cuffs.

Lindsey stared at the blindfold. It was made of the same midnight blue leather as the cuffs on the outside, but the inside was lined with soft black fur. This blindfold was her one soft limit. Her mountain to conquer. But Lindsey had faced her fears with Camilla so many times now. She felt ready.

"You're awfully quiet," Camilla said. "Having second thoughts?"

"No," Lindsey replied. "I want to do this with you."

"I promise I'll take care of you." Camilla slid her own robe from her shoulders. "And I promise I'll make this a pleasurable experience."

She pulled Lindsey close, kissing her with her whole body. The scent of Camilla's freshly washed skin enveloped her. God, everything about her Mistress was mesmerizing. Her long, dark hair, which flowed down her chest, and the way her nipples peeked out from behind it. Her generous curves, which Lindsey just wanted to drown in. Those full, soft lips that made Lindsey weak every time they touched her skin.

Camilla broke away. Silently, she took Lindsey's hand and drew her fingers all the way down Lindsey's arm from her shoulder to her palm. She picked up one of the small cuffs and buckled it around Lindsey's wrist before doing the same with Lindsey's other wrist. Then she took Lindsey's leg and ran her hands down it gently. She straightened out Lindsey's knee, her fingertips tickling the sensitive skin behind it, and buckled a cuff around her ankle carefully. It was like her Mistress was performing some kind of sacred ritual.

Camilla fastened the last cuff around Lindsey's ankle and stood up. "Now for the final touch." She picked up the blindfold and pulled it over Lindsey's head, adjusting it so it sat covering her eyes.

For a moment, Lindsey wanted to panic. The blackness was so complete. But Camilla's presence was enough to ground her. And her anxiousness was far overshadowed by her arousal.

Camilla placed a hand on the front of Lindsey's shoulder. "How does that feel?"

"Good, Mistress," Lindsey said.

"Here." Camilla took Lindsey's hand. "Come with me."

Camilla led Lindsey in the direction of the bed. Lindsey's pulse thrummed in her ears. Was Camilla taking her to the cross? Lindsey's suspicions were confirmed when Camilla nudged her backward, and her shoulder blades hit solid wood.

"Spread your feet apart," Camilla said.

With the same reverence she'd shown earlier, Camilla trailed her hands down each of Lindsey's legs and attached the O-ring of each of the cuffs to the cross. Lindsey couldn't see how she did it, but she heard a metallic click each time. Camilla took Lindsey's wrist and raised her arm up gently, binding it to the cross, then did the same with her other wrist.

Lindsey's breath grew heavy. This was the ultimate surrender. To be bound and helpless, unable to move, and touch, and see. But she wanted this. Lindsey wanted to give herself over to Camilla so completely, to trust her Mistress with every part of herself, to give her all to this woman who made her feel so many incredible things she hadn't even known she was capable of feeling.

Camilla cupped Lindsey's face and kissed her greedily. Lindsey let out a low murmur. The taste of her Mistress's lips was better than fine wine, or chocolate covered strawberries, or any of the other indulgent delights that she'd shared with Camilla.

Camilla drew her fingertips down Lindsey's cheek, down the side of her throat and between her breasts. Her Mistress's feather-light touch made goosebumps form on Lindsey's skin. Soon, Camilla's hands were all over Lindsey's body, painting invisible lines with the pads of her fingers, sculpting Lindsey's curves with her palms.

Right then and there, Lindsey forgot all about the blindfold. All her other senses were overloaded with Camilla. Her touch, her kiss, the scent of her—it flooded every cell in Lindsey's body with need.

"Oh, you like this, don't you?" Camilla traced her thumb over Lindsey's pebbled nipple. "It's not so scary after all, is it?"

"No, Mistress," Lindsey said.

Camilla slid her palm down to Lindsey's mound, skimming her middle finger between Lindsey's outspread lips with an agonizingly light touch. Lindsey pushed her hips out toward Camilla as far as she could.

"Patience." Camilla pressed herself against Lindsey. "I'll give you what you need, but only if you don't rush me, understand?"

"Yes, Mistress," Lindsey whispered.

Camilla broke away. Lindsey waited in silence. Then, she felt a puff of heat on the inside of her thigh. Camilla's breath.

Her Mistress was on her knees.

Lindsey's lips parted, a gust of air escaping them. Camilla had her tied up and at her mercy, yet she offered Lindsey this small act of submission. It paled in comparison to Lindsey's submission. But it filled Lindsey with a desire so insatiable that she felt like she was drowning.

Her Mistress kissed her way up Lindsey's thigh, grabbed onto Lindsey's ass cheeks, and drew her mouth over Lindsey's lower lips. Camilla's lip brushed the side of Lindsey's clit, drawing a sharp hiss from her. With the blindfold keeping Lindsey in darkness, Camilla's every touch was unexpected.

"You can come whenever you want," Camilla said. "I'll be much too busy to give you permission." She swept her hand all the way up Lindsey's leg. "Just enjoy it."

Before Lindsey could say so much as a "Yes, Mistress," Camilla's mouth was between her thighs. She rolled her tongue over Lindsey's folds, from outside to inside, every stroke getting closer and closer to Lindsey's aching bud. Lindsey bit her lip, anticipation growing inside her.

Camilla ran her tongue down to Lindsey's entrance and

dipped it inside. Lindsey's thighs quivered. This slow torture was too much. And the thought of her Mistress on her knees, toying with her restrained body, inflamed her even more.

Finally, Camilla slid her tongue up to Lindsey's clit. Lindsey let out a long, low moan, her muscles growing slack. If she didn't have the cross to hold her up, she would have collapsed into a puddle on the floor.

Camilla worked her mouth between Lindsey's legs, her tongue swirling and her lips sucking. A faint murmur arose from Camilla. The sound vibrated deep into Lindsey's core.

Lindsey trembled. "Mistress!"

One more stroke of Camilla's tongue was all it took to make Lindsey come apart. Her head tipped back as she let out a cry that echoed through the playroom.

When Lindsey stilled, Camilla stood up and crushed her lips against Lindsey's. She lifted the blindfold from Lindsey's eyes. Lindsey had been so lost in ecstasy that she'd forgotten she was even wearing it.

"I'm going to untie you now, okay?" Camilla said.

"Yes, Mistress."

One by one, Camilla unfastened each of the cuffs from the cross, but she didn't remove them from Lindsey's wrists and ankles. She drew Lindsey onto the bed and enveloped her with her arms.

"How are you doing?" Camilla pushed Lindsey's auburn locks out of her face. "Is there anything you need?"

"Mistress," Lindsey said. "The only thing I need right now is you."

She placed her hand on the side of her Mistress's neck and brought her lips to Camilla's. The kiss grew hungrier, more demanding. Lindsey's hands roamed Camilla's body, taking in every part of her with her fingertips. The curve of her cheekbones. The arc of her neck. The dip of her waist, and the mountain of her hip. The soft skin of her inner thighs.

Camilla's breath hitched.

"Mistress," Lindsey said. "May I?"

"Yes," Camilla said. "You can have me. Slowly."

Slowly. Lindsey withdrew her hand and shifted down Camilla's body. She dragged her lips down her Mistress's neck and along her collarbone. A gentle rumble rose from Camilla's chest. Lindsey kissed her way along her Mistress's full breasts and tongued her pebbled peak. Camilla's chest arched up from the bed, pressing herself harder into Lindsey's mouth.

Her lips still on Camilla's nipples, Lindsey snaked her hand down Camilla's stomach, all the way to where her thighs met. Camilla spread them out wide. Lindsey slid her fingers into Camilla's slit. It felt slick and warm under her fingertips.

But what Lindsey really wanted was to taste her again. She crawled all the way down her Mistress's body and parted Camilla's lips with her fingertips. She dipped her head down and licked her all over. Her petal-like folds. Her silky entrance. Her tiny, hidden bud. Lindsey got lost between her Mistress's legs, worshiping the treasure that lay within.

Camilla moaned, her hand falling down to the back of Lindsey's head gently. This wasn't like last time, when Camilla had been firmly in control. This time, Camilla yielded to Lindsey. Sure, Camilla wasn't bound and blindfolded. But Lindsey knew that for her Mistress, this was almost the same thing.

"Oh, Lindsey." Camilla threaded her fingers through Lindsey's hair, holding on tightly. "I'm so close."

Lindsey continued, using everything she could to ravish her Mistress like her Mistress had done to her moments ago. It wasn't long before Camilla let out a gasp, her body quaking as an orgasm took her.

Minutes later, the two of them lay side by side on the bed, totally spent. Lindsey closed her eyes, mumbling wordlessly. She was on another plane, one where nothing existed outside her, and Camilla, and this luxurious bed.

"Lindsey?" Camilla's voice cut through the stillness of the room.

"Mm?"

"I love you."

Something fluttered in Lindsey's chest. When she'd said those words to Camilla, she hadn't expected Camilla to say them back. Just knowing Camilla felt something for her was enough. But hearing her Mistress say those three little words made Lindsey happier than she could have ever imagined.

"I wanted to say it back to you the night of the engagement party, but I was scared."

"Why, Mistress?" Lindsey could tell that this was difficult for Camilla. Maybe it would be easier for her to talk about it as 'Lindsey's Mistress' rather than 'Camilla.'

Camilla shifted on the bed beside her. "Over the course of my life, I've become accustomed to being alone. The truth is, it's easier that way. It means that I don't ever have to worry about being a burden on anyone. I don't have to worry that those close to me will start to resent me for all my limitations."

"I would never consider you a burden," Lindsey said. "And it's obvious that you get along just fine by yourself."

"That's because I've learned to adapt every part of my life around my illness. My carefully regimented routine is a necessity, not a choice. I can't afford to stray from it, to be spontaneous and free. It's restrictive. What happens when it all becomes too much for you?"

"It won't." Lindsey reached for Camilla's hand. "Mistress, neither of us knows what the future holds. All I know is that I want to spend it with you, no matter what."

Camilla was silent. Lindsey turned to look at her. Her eyes were closed and her body was still. The only sign of life was the slow rise and fall of Camilla's chest.

Finally, she spoke. "Do you mean that? That you want to spend the future with me?"

"Yes," Lindsey said. "I do."

"Because our three months is almost up. And ever since the other night, I've been thinking about what comes next."

"So have I. I just didn't know how to bring it up." It was only days since Lindsey had told Camilla she loved her, after all. It had been clear that Camilla was still getting used to the idea. Lindsey hadn't wanted to complicate things further.

"How would you like to move into the manor permanently?" Camilla asked.

Lindsey gaped at her. "Seriously?"

"Seriously. It will be perfect. Nothing will have to change. You can spend your days in the sunroom, working on your art, without having to worry about a thing."

Lindsey let out a wistful sigh. "That does sound perfect. But I wouldn't want to be a kept woman."

Camilla laughed. "A kept woman? Is this the 1920s? Where on earth did you hear a term like that?"

"If you really want to know, it was Denise."

Camilla shook her head. "That's so like her." She placed a hand on Lindsey's shoulder. "You won't be a kept woman. You'll be my girlfriend. My partner. My submissive. So, what do you say?"

"Yes, of course. I would love to stay here with you, Mistress."

"You have no idea how happy that makes me."

Lindsey brought her lips to Camilla's. This was everything she'd ever wanted. Everything she'd ever dreamed of.

Then why did she have this unshakable sense of unease gnawing at her stomach?

CHAPTER TWENTY-ONE

*L*indsey peered over her sketchpad at her Mistress. Camilla lay stretched out along a chaise lounge on her side, wearing nothing but a robe made of pale pink silk. Her straight brown hair flowed down over the arm of the couch, and the afternoon sun streamed through the window behind her, giving her a golden glow.

Lindsey looked back down at her sketchpad. For the last half hour, she'd been trying to draw Camilla. Lindsey wanted to do something nice for her, to give her a gift that was unique and personal. At first, she'd tried to draw Camilla from memory, but she couldn't get it right, so she'd asked Camilla to pose for her.

But even now, Lindsey was struggling. Maybe it was just nerves. This was the first time Lindsey had let Camilla into the sunroom she'd transformed into her studio. And just moments ago, she'd shown Camilla her art for the first time. Lindsey felt like her soul was on display.

Camilla yawned and stretched out her arms. "Christ, is

this what people did before cameras were invented? I should ask June to bring me a bottle of wine."

"Hold still." When Lindsey looked up from her sketchpad again, Camilla was giving her a frosty look. "Sorry! I mean, please hold still, Mistress."

"All right," Camilla said. "Can I talk, at least?"

"Yes, just try not to move too much."

Frowning, Lindsey attempted to fix the shading around Camilla's eyes. How was she supposed to capture the likeness of this larger-than-life woman that she knew so intimately with nothing more than a stick of charcoal and a piece of paper?

"I was thinking some more about the future," Camilla said. "About us, and you. Have you thought about making a career of your art?

"I don't know," Lindsey murmured.

"Isn't that what you always wanted to do with your life?"

"I guess." Lindsey paused, her charcoal poised above the page. "But I have all those bills to pay off."

Camilla propped herself up on one elbow. "Darling, I was always going to give you the money to cover your medical bills. That hasn't changed now that we're actually in a relationship. You don't have to worry about that anymore."

Camilla had a point. Lindsey didn't have any reason not to pursue her dreams. She felt a surge of anxiety. "I don't know if I'm ready for that yet."

"Are you really not ready? Or are you just afraid?"

Lindsey didn't answer.

"You've shown me your work, Lindsey. You have real talent. I know good art when I see it, and yours is wonderful. It would be a shame to hide it from the rest of the world."

"Maybe you're right."

"Well, if you decide you want to put yourself out there, I have a friend who owns a gallery in the city. If you put together a portfolio, I can show it to her."

"I wouldn't want to take advantage of your connections," Lindsey said.

"You wouldn't be. My friend is always looking for works by fresh talent. And she's merciless when it comes to anything that isn't to her taste. She won't hesitate to turn you down if she doesn't like your work. But I know she'll love it."

"Can I think about it?"

"Sure." Camilla settled back onto the chaise.

Lindsey stared at her sketchpad and sighed. This was all wrong. If she couldn't even draw a simple sketch of Camilla, how was she supposed to create something worthy of showing in a gallery?

"Are you okay?" Camilla asked.

"I'm just struggling with this, that's all," Lindsey said. "Maybe we should do this another time."

Camilla sat up. "Come here, Lindsey."

Lindsey placed her sketchbook on the chair and slunk over to sit next to Camilla.

Camilla draped an arm around Lindsey and pulled her close. "I'm sorry, I didn't mean to pressure you."

"It's not that. I'm just having an off day."

"You do seem tense. How about we do something else instead?" Camilla's voice dropped to a seductive whisper. "Something to help you relax."

Lindsey smiled. "Like what, Mistress?"

"Like have a little fun in the playroom together."

Lindsey glanced at the clock. It was mid-afternoon. "Don't you have to work?"

"Last time I checked, I was in charge. I can do whatever I want. And right now, what I want is you." Camilla drew Lindsey in close and kissed her, hard. "Playroom. Now."

"Relax." Camilla brushed her fingers along Lindsey's bare back. "You're still too tense."

Lindsey murmured into the pillow. She was lying naked on her stomach on the playroom bed, the cuffs around her wrists and ankles and the blindfold covering her eyes. Camilla was in the middle of giving her what could only be described as a kinky massage.

Camilla's hands were replaced by long, thin tails that swept across Lindsey's back. It had to be a flogger. She shivered, her muscles loosening. The leather strips tickled her skin.

"That's much better," Camilla said.

She flicked the flogger against Lindsey's back, first gently, then a little harder, ramping up the intensity with each strike. Lindsey moaned with bliss, letting the smacks resonate through her body. She was starting to enter that space where everything outside of her seemed to fall away.

"Are you feeling more relaxed now?" Camilla asked.

"Yes, Mistress." Lindsey's sensitized skin tingled pleasantly, and there was a faint scent of something sweet and floral in the air.

"Then it's time for the fun to really begin."

Lindsey reveled in her powerlessness. The cuffs around her ankles and wrists weren't attached to anything, so she wasn't restrained in any way. However, being blindfolded still made Lindsey feel on edge, and she found that rush almost as addictive as Camilla herself.

"Stay perfectly still," her Mistress said.

Camilla's footsteps receded from the bed. Lindsey listened carefully, but she couldn't hear a thing. She took a deep breath, and froze.

The sweet scent that had filled the room had been replaced by something else. Something smoky, like burning oil. It hung so thick in the air that Lindsey couldn't breathe. Suddenly, the cuffs around her ankles and wrists felt tight and restricting, and the darkness shrouding her seemed to swallow her up. She was trapped, unable to move, the smell of fuel and smoke from a fire she couldn't see-

"Lindsey?" Her Mistress's clear voice cut through her nightmare.

"Apple," Lindsey whispered.

At once, Camilla was on the bed with her, tearing off the blindfold. Lindsey opened her eyes to see her Mistress staring back at her.

"Are you all right?" Although Camilla tried to hide it, there was a hint of panic in her voice.

Lindsey nodded, blinking against the light. She sat up. On the nightstand next to her were two lit candles. Candles, the kind used to drip hot wax on someone's skin. That's what the smell was. Now, it smelled nothing like burning fuel. Lindsey's brain had made that part up on its own.

Camilla grabbed a thick blanket from the end of the bed

and draped it around Lindsey's shoulders. Lindsey shivered and pulled it tight. Her heart was finally slowing down to normal.

"What's the matter?" Camilla asked.

"I'm sorry," Lindsey said quietly. Camilla seemed hesitant to touch her. But considering how erratically she was behaving, Lindsey didn't blame her.

"Don't be sorry. Just tell me what's going on."

"I didn't know that was going to happen. I thought I was okay with being blindfolded and all the other stuff, but I've just been feeling so off, and-" Lindsey's lip quivered. "I'm sorry."

Camilla wrapped her arms around Lindsey and pulled her in close. "Lindsey, it's fine. You used your safeword. That's a good thing. And even if you hadn't, I could tell something was wrong. Do you want to tell me what all this is about?"

Lindsey hesitated. "It was just, the darkness and the smell of smoke. It reminded me of the car accident I was in. I've been jumpy about certain things since then. Long car rides. Driving at night. Smoke, apparently, too."

"It sounds like what you went through was difficult," Camilla said.

Lindsey shrugged. "I guess."

"Have you talked to anyone about it?"

"Not really."

"Do you want to talk about it?"

"I don't know," Lindsey said. "I feel like I'm making a big deal out of nothing. Lots of people get into car accidents. I walked away from it fine in the end. Plus, it was all my fault."

"Why do you say that?" Camilla asked.

"It happened when I was driving across the country to my parents' house at the very end of senior year." Underneath the blanket, Lindsey brought her hand up to the scar on her collarbone. "I'd basically spent the whole week drinking and partying. I was sober by the time I started driving, but I was really tired. I was on this long stretch of highway, without any streetlights, and there wasn't a car in sight. I don't know what happened exactly, but the next thing I knew, my car had gone off the road and I'd hit a tree.

"I hit my head in the crash, and when I came to, the lights had gone out, and it was dark, so I couldn't see anything. And I was trapped in the car, and I couldn't move. But I could smell smoke, and all I could think about was that the car was about to burst into flames and I'd die there, all alone, trapped in the dark."

"Lindsey, that must have been awful."

"That's the thing," Lindsey said. "I wasn't really in any danger, I just thought I was. Cars don't explode like they do in movies. I looked it up afterward. It doesn't happen."

Camilla rubbed her hand along Lindsey's arm. "You didn't know that."

"That doesn't make me feel like any less of an idiot for panicking over nothing. I don't even know how long I was trapped in my car for, but it felt like forever. Eventually, a woman drove past and called 911. She stayed with me until help came. They had to cut me out of the car. I ended up with a concussion and some broken bones. Apparently, I was lucky that I wasn't injured more seriously. I had a handful of surgeries and got out of the hospital after only a couple of weeks, but I had to do physical therapy for my broken femur for months afterward. I ended up moving back across the country to live with my parents while I recovered."

Camilla stroked Lindsey's arm. "That must have been hard."

"It was," Lindsey said. "But what came next was even harder. After I recovered, it felt like the whole world had changed. I moved back here, but all my friends from art school had moved on without me. I felt so anxious, and lost, and alone, but it was more than that. I'd changed. I just wasn't the same person I used to be."

"That's not surprising," Camilla said. "What you went through sounds pretty traumatic. It would make anyone anxious. And those kinds of experiences can change you."

"But no one ever tells you how to deal with that. Once your bones are healed, you're just thrown out into the world and expected to get on with life. But how are you supposed to do that? How are you supposed to go back to being the person you were before everything? And how do you make people understand why you feel that way?"

"Oh, Lindsey." Camilla hugged her tighter. "I understand what that's like. To have something life changing happen to you and have everyone just expect you to get on with it."

"Huh," Lindsey said. "I guess you've been through this."

"Well, it wasn't exactly the same. But when the symptoms of my illness started, I was fourteen. No one knew what was going on, and no one knew how to help me. That went on for years. And when the doctors finally figured out what was causing everything, there was very little they could do. I was basically just told to get on with things. But how could I do that when I'd been stuck with this diagnosis that was going to affect me every day for the rest of my life? How could I go back to being that carefree teenager when my future had been changed irrevocably?"

"Yes, that's exactly it." Lindsey paused. "How did you deal with that?"

"Well, eventually, I ended up seeing a new doctor who insisted I get therapy," Camilla said. "It helped. My therapist told me that it was okay to grieve for the life that I once had, for the old me. That it was okay to feel lost and hopeless sometimes. That I didn't have to pretend that everything was okay all the time. And she taught me how to deal with all those feelings. You should consider seeing someone too."

"I've never been able to afford it," Lindsey said.

"You can now. I'll pay for it. And if you don't want to talk to a stranger, you can always talk to me. Whenever you need me, I'll be right here."

"Thanks." Lindsey gave Camilla a reserved smile. "I don't know why I never thought to talk to you about it. I'm just so used to pretending it's not a problem."

Camilla kissed Lindsey on the forehead. "Well, you don't have to pretend with me. I don't want there to be anything between us that we can't talk about."

Right. Lindsey's stomach tightened. This was why she'd been feeling uneasy. Despite everything that had passed between them, Lindsey was still hiding something from Camilla. She still hadn't told Camilla that she'd never been attracted to another woman before her.

But how was she supposed to tell Camilla that their relationship began with a lie?

CHAPTER TWENTY-TWO

Lindsey lay on Camilla's bed, a book in her hand. It was Lindsey's bed now, too. She'd been sleeping in it every night since Denise came to visit, but Camilla had asked Lindsey to 'move in' after their conversation the other night. Lindsey had said yes, but she still felt like an intruder. It didn't help that Camilla was away for work again. At least it was only for a few days this time. She was due back tomorrow night.

Lindsey gazed out the window at the night sky. Here Camilla was, planning their future together, yet Lindsey was still stuck on the lie she'd told Camilla the day they'd met. Lindsey wanted to tell her. But she didn't know how. And Lindsey didn't want to hurt her.

Maybe it would be better for her to take the secret to her grave.

Lindsey put down her book and got up from the bed. Being alone in this big house, with no one but her thoughts for company, was starting to get to her. Faith was due to call for a chat when she got home from work, but that wasn't for a few hours. Lindsey left Camilla's room and made her way downstairs in search of a snack.

She entered the main kitchen. It was empty at the moment, and every surface was sparkling clean. Lindsey had only been in here a handful of times. If she wanted something to eat, she usually asked June. But what Lindsey was really looking for was a distraction.

She opened the door to the walk-in pantry and began searching the shelves. It was like a tiny grocery store in itself. She found a few shelves in the back that were full of all those sweet, indulgent snacks that Camilla liked to eat. After browsing the selection for a few minutes, Lindsey picked out a block of dark chocolate and took it over to the island in the middle of the kitchen. She sat down and broke off a few squares, munching on them idly.

"Lindsey? Do you need something?"

Lindsey turned to see June at the door, a bucket of cleaning supplies in her hand.

"I was just looking for a snack." She held up the block of chocolate.

"Do you want something more substantial? I can make you anything you want."

"No, it's fine." Lindsey hesitated. "But I could use some company."

June put down the bucket and leaned against the bench across from Lindsey. "This place feels empty without her, doesn't it? She's like the lifeblood of this house."

"She is." Lindsey held out the block of chocolate to June, who broke off a small square.

"I'm glad the two of you found each other," June said.

"Lord knows Camilla could use someone to take care of her."

"Are we talking about the same person? Camilla doesn't exactly need taking care of."

"That's not what I meant." June pulled up a chair and sat down. "I have no doubt that if Camilla went bankrupt tomorrow, and if all of her friends disappeared, she'd still find a way to single-handedly claw her way back up to where she is now. She doesn't need anyone else to survive. But it's a very lonely existence when all you do is survive."

That much was true. Lindsey had been living like that ever since the accident. Sleepwalking her way through each day, lost in a fog of anxiety and listlessness.

That was, until she met Camilla.

"I guess you're right," Lindsey said. "You seem to know Camilla pretty well."

June reached over to break off another piece of chocolate. "I've known her for 20 years. Her parents hired me, but after they passed away, Camilla kept me on and promoted me to head housekeeper. I've worked for her every day since then."

"Every day?"

"Well, I take the occasional vacation. Camilla tries to make me take more, but it's hard for me to leave this place. I have a connection to it. Camilla might be the lifeblood of the house, but I'm the brain."

"Keeping this place running seems like a lot of work," Lindsey said.

"It is. But the job comes with a lot of perks. Like the pay. I'm not even fifty, and I have enough money to retire tomorrow and never work again. Plus, Camilla's been taking care of my parents. They both have health problems, so they need round the clock care. Camilla pays for them to live in a world-class care facility."

"Wow, that's generous of her."

"Are you that surprised?" June said. "I thought you'd have her figured out by now."

"What do you mean?" Lindsey asked.

"Well, we both know how prickly Camilla can be on the outside, but she's got a good heart. She shows her love by helping out others, usually in the most outrageous of ways. And not just with money. She'll march into your life, fix all your problems, and make sure all your needs are taken care of, whether you want her to or not."

Yep. That was Camilla all over.

"That's why she needs someone like you," June said. "Someone who will let her pretend that she's your rock when in reality, you're the one who will quietly be there for her without letting her know it."

Lindsey rested her chin on her hands. It was true that Camilla seemed happiest when she was making other people happy. And whenever Camilla was unwell or felt stressed, all she wanted was to hold Lindsey and smother her with affection like Lindsey was the one who needed comforting.

June stood up and tucked her chair neatly under the kitchen island. "I better get back to work. This house has to be spotless when Camilla gets back. You know how your Mistress gets when things aren't up to her standards." She reached over to take one last piece of chocolate. "At least she doesn't make me write lines."

Heat rose up Lindsey's face. As June left the room,

Lindsey buried her head in her hands. She shouldn't have been surprised that June was so sharp. She'd have to be to have survived in this house with Camilla for 20 years.

Lindsey grabbed the rest of the chocolate and made her way back up the stairs. When she reached the top, she paused. Instead of going toward Camilla's rooms, Lindsey went back to her old bedroom. She felt a little more comfortable there. And she knew she wouldn't feel welcome in Camilla's rooms until she'd dealt with the problem that was causing her guilt.

She flopped down on her bed and put in her headphones, blasting some music through them. Being in a little cocoon of sound usually helped take her mind off things. Lindsey shut her eyes. Before she knew it, she was drifting off to sleep.

Lindsey woke with a start. Her phone was buzzing on her chest and the room was pitch black. She yawned. How long had she been asleep for?

Lindsey sat up and answered her phone. "Hey, Faith."

"Hi," Faith said cheerfully. "Sorry I took so long to call you. I had to stay back and have an awkward conversation with the mom I work for."

"Oh, is everything okay?"

"Yeah. My pay was late, but she assured me they'd pay me tomorrow. How are you?"

"I'm okay. A little bored. Camilla is away again."

"Is that why you wanted to talk?" Faith asked. "Feeling all lovesick because you can't bear to be apart from her for a few days?"

"It's not that." Lindsey took one of the giant cushions from her bed and hugged it to her chest. "We've been talking about the future. About me moving in with her. Permanently."

Faith let out a squeal. "That's great. You said you're in it for the long run with her, right? And that the manor feels like home now?"

"Yeah. I want this. But I can't help but feel bad about how everything between us started."

"What, because you were her sugar baby? Who cares if everything was fake at the beginning? You're not faking it anymore."

"Well, yeah," Lindsey said. "But I lied to her about being interested in women when we first met. Or at least, I led her to believe I was, which is basically the same thing."

"Right," Faith said. "So you haven't told her yet?"

"Nope. And I've had so many opportunities to tell her the truth, but I didn't. She's been so open with me about everything. I feel awful about keeping this from her."

"Then tell her."

"I don't want to hurt her," Lindsey said. "She's going to feel so betrayed. What if she can't forgive me?"

"What choice do you have?" Faith asked. "Do you really think the two of you can be happy together with this cloud hanging over your relationship?"

Lindsey sighed. "You're right. I'll tell her when she gets back." She let herself fall back down onto the pillows. "I hope she takes it well. Because if she doesn't, I don't know what I'll do. I love her so much, Faith. I never thought I'd fall for another woman, let alone one so much older than me, but here I am. Whenever I'm with her, I feel like I'm having this wonderful, impossible dream. But it's real."

"Aw, Lindsey. I'm glad you found this little slice of

happiness. And for the record, I don't think your feelings for Camilla were fake at the start. You were practically swooning after that first date with her. From the outside, your feelings always seemed real, even if you didn't realize it at the time."

"I think you're right," Lindsey said. "Maybe I was falling for her all along, but I didn't understand it yet."

It was another hour before they hung up. By then, it was late. Lindsey put her phone aside and got ready for bed. She would talk to Camilla about everything tomorrow night.

She just hoped that Camilla would understand.

CHAPTER TWENTY-THREE

The next morning, Lindsey bounded out of her rooms and down the stairs. Making the decision to tell Camilla the truth had lifted a huge weight from her shoulders. Lindsey knew it would be a difficult conversation. She knew Camilla would be hurt. But she had to have faith that Camilla would forgive her.

She entered the dining room. There was no sign of June, but breakfast was laid out for Lindsey as usual. She finished it off quickly and headed back up to her rooms to brush her teeth. It was a warm, sunny day outside. Perhaps she'd go for a swim.

When she reached her rooms, she found June waiting for her by the door. The housekeeper's face wore a grave expression. A chill rolled down Lindsey's neck.

Something was wrong.

"June?" she said. "What's the matter?"

June folded her hands in front of her apron. "Camilla has requested that you leave the estate."

All warmth drained from Lindsey's body. "What are you talking about?"

"You need to pack your things. A car will be coming to take you wherever you want to go."

"This doesn't make any sense." Slowly, June's words began to sink in. "Why would Camilla do this? I need to talk to her."

"That isn't possible," June said.

"She's coming back tonight, right? Can't I wait for her?"

There was a flicker of confusion behind June's eyes. "Didn't the two of you-" she stopped short.

"June," Lindsey said. "What's going on?"

"Camilla already came back. Last night."

Lindsey's heart turned to ice. Last night, when she'd spoken to Faith about the secret she'd kept from Camilla?

"Where's Camilla now?" Lindsey asked.

"I can't tell you that," June said. "And her instructions were clear. You're to leave as soon as you've packed your things."

"You have to tell me where she is, June."

"I can't tell you where she is, because I don't *know* where she is. She left again early in the morning. I assumed she wanted space."

No. This wasn't happening.

"A car will arrive for you shortly. You better start packing. I'm also to inform you that anything Camilla bought for you is yours to take with you."

"I don't want her things!" Lindsey said. "I want to talk to her. June, please!"

"I'm sorry," June said quietly. "There's nothing I can do." Without another word, she turned and walked away.

Lindsey entered her room in a daze. This was all wrong. Lindsey needed to see her, to tell Camilla that she loved her, and she was sorry for lying.

She sank down into an armchair. Would it even make a difference? Camilla was so mad at Lindsey that she was kicking her out of the manor without even giving her a chance to explain herself.

Camilla wasn't a forgiving woman. She would never forgive Lindsey, not after this. She had trusted Lindsey, had let her in, and Lindsey had betrayed that trust.

Did Lindsey even deserve her forgiveness?

She could stay here, in this chair, and refuse to leave. She could insist on waiting for Camilla. She could cry and scream until Camilla came running.

But there was no point.

Lindsey got up and pulled her suitcase out of the closet. She looked around at all the clothes, shoes, and accessories Camilla had bought her. June had said they were hers to keep. But Lindsey didn't want any of it. Not without Camilla.

There was a knock on the door.

"Come in," Lindsey said.

June entered the room and pulled an envelope from a pocket at the front of her apron. "I forgot to give this to you. It's from Camilla."

Lindsey stared at the envelope. Was it a note? A letter? Some kind of explanation or a goodbye?

June held it out to her. "Here."

Lindsey blinked and took the envelope. "Thanks, June."

But June didn't give Lindsey her usual polite nod. She

simply left the room again. Lindsey tore open the envelope, her hands trembling.

It was a check made out to Lindsey, for the exact amount Camilla had promised her before she'd moved in.

Lindsey collapsed onto her knees and started to sob.

Lindsey lay curled up on Faith's couch, tissues strewn around her. She'd called Faith in tears after leaving the manor. She had no one else to turn to, nowhere to go. Faith still had a few hours before she finished work, so Lindsey was all alone. At least she still had Faith's spare key.

The sound of the front door opening reached Lindsey's ears. She didn't bother to look. She didn't have the energy to move or do anything other than try to keep herself from bursting into tears.

"Lindsey? I'm home." Faith's footsteps approached. She sat down on the couch next to Lindsey's head. "How are you doing?"

Before Lindsey could answer her, she started sobbing into Faith's lap.

"Oh honey," Faith said. "I'm sorry."

"I messed up. I messed up so badly, and she'll never forgive me, and now it's over." Lindsey felt a wrenching in her chest. "I didn't know I could hurt this much. It's like my insides are filled with all these tiny shards of glass and it hurts to even breathe."

"I know." Faith stroked Lindsey's head. "This is what a broken heart feels like."

Lindsey sniffled. "Is it always this bad?"

"Every time."

"Then why do people do this? Why do people fall in love when this is what always happens?"

"Because when you finally find the person you're meant to be with, all of that past heartbreak is worth it. At least, I hope that's the case. For both of our sakes."

Another round of sobs racked Lindsey's body. "But *she* was the person I was meant to be with."

"It will get better," Faith said. "I promise. It'll take a while, but it'll start to hurt less. You'll be okay in the end."

"No, I won't. I'll never be okay again. Not after I hurt her so badly."

"Don't be so hard on yourself. You'll get through this. And I'll be right here with you."

Lindsey wiped her eyes. "Wait, why are you here? I thought you didn't finish work until this evening?"

"The Yangs let me go after I picked the kids up from school. There's a reason they've been paying me late. It turns out they can't afford a nanny anymore."

"I'm sorry, Faith."

Faith shrugged. "They said they'd give me a good reference. Maybe I'll find some other rich family to nanny for. On the plus side, it means I'll be around to keep you company." She sighed. "I really liked that job, though."

"I guess we can be miserable together," Lindsey said.

"Should I make some punch?"

"God, no." Still, Lindsey couldn't help but smile.

"You see?" Faith said. "Things aren't all doom and gloom. It'll be okay."

CHAPTER TWENTY-FOUR

Lindsey lay on Faith's couch, staring at the ceiling. An old sitcom was playing on the TV, but Lindsey wasn't paying attention to it. How was she supposed to do something as mundane as watch TV when she felt like her heart had been torn right out of her chest?

Ever since the accident, Lindsey had been struggling to feel anything at all. It was why she'd agreed to do something this crazy in the first place. She'd wanted adventure, romance, to capture that feeling of being happy and carefree.

She had gotten so much more than that. She'd stopped living in the past, stopped looking backward, and started looking forward to the future that she was supposed to share with Camilla. She'd fallen in love for the first time.

And now she felt the crushing pain of heartbreak.

There was a knock on the door. Lindsey groaned. She didn't want to get up. She'd barely left the couch for the past few days, with the exception of this morning. Faith had forced her to take a shower, because, in Faith's words,

Lindsey was 'getting stinky.' But Faith was out running errands, leaving Lindsey all alone in the house again.

There was another knock on the door, more insistent this time. Lindsey sighed and got up. Her muscles protested, but whoever this was wasn't going away.

Lindsey reached the front door and opened it wide. She froze.

It was Camilla.

Lindsey stared at her. She looked so different. This wasn't the warm, bright-eyed Camilla who had told Lindsey she loved her. It was the Camilla who had looked at her, stone-faced, that night Lindsey had sneaked into her rooms so long ago.

But this was so much worse.

Seconds passed, and neither of them said a word. Lindsey smoothed down her hair, self-conscious under Camilla's sharp gaze. Barefoot and in her sweats, Lindsey was sure she looked like a mess. Suddenly, she was grateful that Faith had made her take a shower.

Finally, Camilla held out an envelope. "Take it."

Lindsey stared at the envelope. It had already been opened, and it looked familiar. It was the check. The check that June had given her.

The check that Lindsey had left behind, sitting on the dresser in her old room, along with all the clothes and fancy things Camilla had bought her.

Camilla thrust the envelope at Lindsey. "Take it."

"I'm not taking it," Lindsey said.

"Why not?"

"Because I don't want it."

"This was the agreement." Camilla's voice was hard. "I'm

just holding up my end of it."

"Our agreement?" Lindsey shook her head. "What are you talking about?"

"This is what you wanted, wasn't it? The money? That was the whole point of this."

"Well, yes, at first. But that obviously changed when I fell in love with you."

"Don't say that. Don't lie to me."

"It's not a lie," Lindsey said. "I love you, Mistress."

"Lindsey, stop. I know the truth. I heard you talking on the phone. You were never interested in women. You've been lying to me from the start. Why would you pretend you were in love with me if not for the money?"

Lindsey flinched. "All this time, that's what you thought? That I lied about being in love with you?" She thought back to her conversation with Faith. It would have been easy for Camilla to come to that conclusion if she'd overheard only part of it from the other side of a door. "That's why you kicked me out?"

"It's the truth," Camilla said.

"No, it's not. You need to let me explain. Just come in, so we can talk about this."

Camilla pressed her lips together. "There's nothing to talk about. Just take the damn check."

"You know what? Fine. I'll take it." Lindsey took the envelope from Camilla's hand. She pulled out the check and tore it in half.

Camilla gaped at her. "What are you doing?"

Lindsey tore the check in half again, and again, over and over until it was in a billion tiny pieces which she sprinkled on the floor at Camilla's feet.

"Why did you do that?"

"Why do you think?" Lindsey said. "I told you I don't care about the money. It's you that I want. Just hear me out. Give me five minutes to explain myself."

"Fine," Camilla said sharply. "Five minutes."

Lindsey opened the door and let Camilla in. Camilla followed her to the living room. Lindsey swept aside the candy bar wrappers and chip packets on the couch and gestured for her to sit down.

"Camilla. Mistress, I-" Lindsey took a breath, gathering her thoughts. "You're right. I lied to you. When we met, I pretended I was bisexual. That I liked women. That was a lie. I'd never been with a woman, never been attracted to one. Not until I met you."

Camilla said nothing. Her expression remained unchanged.

"From the moment I met you, I felt this incredible connection to you. I didn't understand what it was at the time because it was like nothing else I'd ever felt. I just wanted so badly to be near you, to be a part of your life, even though I couldn't explain it. That's why I agreed to your proposal. Sure, the money was part of it. But what I really wanted was to get to know you.

"And over those months we spent together, I got to know what an incredible woman you are," Lindsey said. "I got to know how strong you are. How kind and generous you are. How loyal and loving you are toward the people you care about. And in just a couple of short months, I fell in love with you. And even before I did, I stopped caring about the money. The moment you kissed me in the playroom that first night, I was yours."

Something flickered behind Camilla's eyes. A tiny spark of affection, a hint of longing. Camilla felt it too. Lindsey knew it.

"So yes, this started with a lie," she said. "But that was the only lie I ever told you. Every time I said I was yours, I meant it. Every time I said I miss you, I meant it. Every time I said I love you, I meant it. And I still do. That's the truth."

Lindsey folded her hands in her lap and waited for Camilla to do or say something. For what seemed like an eternity, all she did was stare back at Lindsey, an unreadable expression on her face.

"You really mean that," Camilla said.

"Of course I do, or I wouldn't have said it. I love you," Lindsey said. "I love you. I love you. I love-"

Camilla held up her hands. "Lindsey, stop."

Lindsey fell silent. There was nothing more for her to say. If Camilla wasn't convinced now, then all was lost.

"I love you too, Lindsey."

Relief flooded Lindsey's body. She threw her arms around Camilla's neck and kissed her as hard as she could. Camilla's hungry lips were as sweet and soft as ever, and her Mistress's strong embrace filled her with warmth.

Camilla drew back. "Come home, Lindsey."

Home. Lindsey looked around Faith's small apartment, at the couch littered with tissues and her suitcase in the corner. Although this place had been good to Lindsey, it was never going to be home.

But the manor? That was home. And it always would be, as long as Camilla was there.

"Yes, Mistress. I'll come home."

CHAPTER TWENTY-FIVE

That afternoon, Lindsey and Camilla returned to Robinson Estate. As soon as they passed through those wide gates, Lindsey was transported back to that little slice of paradise that belonged to Lindsey and her Mistress, and no one else.

When they reached the manor, Camilla went about making Lindsey's homecoming as perfect as their first night together. She called in a chef and gave Lindsey a new dress, a knee-length number made of delicate black chiffon which Camilla had bought to surprise Lindsey the night she'd returned early. They had dinner in the garden, complete with a dessert decadent enough to satisfy Camilla's sweet tooth. Then they relaxed in the courtyard under the soft lights and the stars.

Lindsey would have been happy to end the night simply falling asleep next to Camilla. But Camilla had bigger plans.

"I have one final gift to give you," Camilla said. "It's inside."

Lindsey followed Camilla back into the house and

through the white double doors that led to Camilla's rooms. Camilla stopped at the playroom door and led Lindsey inside.

Despite the fact that last time Lindsey had been in here, she'd had a bad experience, the playroom still felt cozy and welcoming. As usual, the wooden chest was sitting on top of the table. Camilla opened it up, pulled out the cuffs, and fastened them around Lindsey's wrists and ankles.

"Now for the final piece." Camilla placed her hand on Lindsey's shoulder. "Kneel."

Lindsey kneeled down on the fluffy rug. Her Mistress's serious tone sent a thrill through her.

Camilla reached into the box again and produced a leather collar. It was made of the same embossed midnight blue leather as the cuffs around Lindsey's ankles and wrists. Hanging from a ring at the front was a little gold tag with Camilla's initials on it.

Camilla leaned down and swept Lindsey's hair to the side. Then, holding the collar as gingerly as if it were a precious diamond necklace, she fastened it around Lindsey's neck, securing it at the back with the gold buckle.

"Rise," Camilla said.

Lindsey stood up. The soft collar fit snugly around her neck, and the weight of the leather and gold was just hefty enough to remind her that it was there.

Camilla tipped Lindsey's chin up to inspect the collar. "You look radiant."

She hooked a finger into the ring at the front of the collar and pulled Lindsey toward her, kissing her feverishly. It took all Lindsey's strength not to crumble to pieces.

Still holding the collar, Camilla tugged her toward the bed. "Stand in front of the cross."

Lindsey did as she was told, anticipation welling inside her. Last time Camilla had tied her to the cross, the experience had been divine.

"Not that way," Camilla said. "Face it."

Lindsey turned around. Camilla fastened Lindsey to the cross by her wrists and ankles, leaving her spread-eagled, her back exposed. Lindsey's heart raced.

Camilla brushed her fingers down the back of Lindsey's upstretched arm. "I'm not going to blindfold you. This time, you're going to keep your eyes closed. Can you do that for me?"

"Yes, Mistress." Lindsey shut her eyes.

Camilla planted a kiss on Lindsey's cheek. Her hands glided down Lindsey's sides, caressing her helpless body. "Let's get this dress out of the way."

Camilla's footsteps receded behind Lindsey. What was she doing? It was going to be impossible for Camilla to remove Lindsey's dress with her limbs bound as they were.

Her Mistress returned to her side. Suddenly, there was a metallic swish behind Lindsey's ear, then the bite of cold metal between her shoulder blades. *Scissors?* Lindsey's eyes tried to fly open, but she resisted the impulse. Then, she heard a sharp snip as the blade slid down the bare skin of her back.

Camilla was cutting off Lindsey's dress.

Heat suffused Lindsey's body. If she wasn't so turned on, she would have laughed at how outrageous it was. Her Mistress had gifted her this beautiful dress, just to ruin it a few hours later.

Camilla snipped all the way down to the hem at the bottom, cutting the dress in half completely, then snipped the straps at her shoulders. She yanked the dress out from between Lindsey's body and the cross, then cut away her bra and panties, piece by piece. The back of the scissors scraped Lindsey's skin, sending shivers down her neck.

Soon, Lindsey was left wearing nothing but the collar and cuffs.

"That's much better," Camilla said. "Now I can admire all of you."

Camilla turned Lindsey's head to one side and brought her lips to Lindsey's. Camilla's deep, yearning kiss flooded Lindsey with lust. And the way Camilla's body pressed against her back made Lindsey realize that Camilla was no longer wearing anything.

Suddenly, keeping her eyes closed was a much more difficult prospect.

"You're turned on already, aren't you?" Camilla said. "If I stuck my hand between your thighs, would I find you soaking wet?"

"Yes, Mistress," Lindsey replied.

"But I'm not going to do that yet. Not when I have you stretched out on display for me like this." Camilla spanked Lindsey across the ass cheek. "I'm going to have some fun with you instead."

Lindsey let out a shallow breath. She had a few guesses as to what Camilla had in mind. Lindsey was immobilized and naked, her bare ass right in the center of the X. It was the perfect target.

Lindsey felt something long and hard sweep along the back of her thigh. She stiffened.

"Remember this?" Camilla asked.

"Yes, Mistress." How could Lindsey forget the cane that Camilla had used on her that first night?

Camilla traced the cane up Lindsey's ass cheek. "This time, you're going to thank me for every strike. Do you understand?"

"Yes, Mistress."

Camilla stepped back. There were a few loud whooshes as Camilla swung the cane through the air. Lindsey waited for the impact, but none came. She wriggled impatiently.

"You're not trying to tempt me, are you?" Camilla asked.

"No, Mistress," Lindsey said.

"I think you are. Maybe some discipline will stop you being such a naughty little submissive."

There was a loud whoosh, then the white-hot strike of the cane against Lindsey's ass cheeks. She hissed.

"What do you say?" Camilla asked.

"Thank you, Mistress," Lindsey said.

Camilla swatted her again.

"Thank you, Mistress."

Again. This time, the searing sensation radiated through her whole body, to the tips of her fingers and toes, and into her core.

Thank you, Mistress. Thank you, Mistress. Over and over until every part of Lindsey ached with need. She moaned, her mind and body falling into a blissful trance. *Thank you, Mistress. Thank you, Mistress.*

Camilla ran a hand down the center of Lindsey's back. "Are you still with me?"

"Yes, Mistress," Lindsey said softly.

Camilla skimmed her hand downward, between Lindsey's ass cheeks and into her slit. Lindsey let out a hard breath.

"Do not come without asking for permission," Camilla said.

"Yes-" Lindsey gasped as Camilla's finger grazed the base of her clit. "Yes, Mistress."

Without hesitation, Camilla slipped her fingers inside Lindsey, plunging deep. Lindsey whimpered. She was so delightfully on edge that it was only seconds before she was ready.

"Please, Mistress. Can I come?"

"Not yet." Camilla slowed down slightly.

Lindsey's head fell back. There was no way she could last any longer. "I can't…"

"You can. For me." Camilla pushed Lindsey's hair aside and kissed and sucked behind her ear and down to the collar around her neck. Her free hand crept between Lindsey's body and the cross, all the way up to her chest.

Lindsey strained against her bonds, flexing her muscles. Somehow, despite Camilla's fingers thrusting inside her, and her lips on her skin, Lindsey held herself back from the edge. Somehow, despite being tormented with ecstasy, she kept her word to her Mistress. Lindsey was hers so completely that both her mind and body understood that it couldn't have true release without her Mistress's permission.

"Now." Camilla began moving her hand faster. "You may come."

Lindsey let out a primal cry as pleasure burst from within her, spreading through her like wildfire. Camilla kept her body pressed against Lindsey's as she worked her fingers inside, until Lindsey's body calmed.

"You can open your eyes now," Camilla said.

Lindsey opened her eyes, turning to watch her Mistress as she unfastened the restraints from the cross. Once Lindsey was free, her Mistress drew her to the bed and climbed onto it, lying back against the pillows.

Taking Lindsey by the ring of the collar again, she pulled Lindsey down to her. Wordlessly, their lips locked together, and their arms intertwined. Camilla's thigh brushed between Lindsey's legs. She rocked her hips on top of Camilla, burning with desire.

Camilla shifted out from under her, pulling Lindsey down so that they were side by side. She drew her hand up to the peak of Lindsey's thighs and strummed her aching bud. Lindsey pressed back against her Mistress. At the same time, she pushed her own fingers down to where Camilla's thighs met and slipped them gently up her folds. Camilla moaned and grabbed onto Lindsey's hand, guiding it to her entrance.

Lindsey got the message loud and clear. She eased a finger inside Camilla, delving it in and out slowly. A ripple went through Camilla's body. She arched toward Lindsey, a wordless command. *More.* Lindsey slid in another finger, eliciting a murmur of satisfaction from Camilla. Her walls seemed to swallow Lindsey's fingers. She pumped in and out again, getting into a rhythm, sinking into her Mistress's heat.

Camilla grabbed Lindsey's face and kissed her like a woman starved. Her other hand was still between Lindsey's lower lips, circling and stroking. Lindsey bucked against her. She was so close. She opened her mouth to beg for release.

But instead, it was her Mistress who was overcome. Camilla quaked against Lindsey, her head tipped back in a silent scream. Lindsey could feel every pulse that went through her Mistress's core, every shudder that went through her Mistress's body. It only made Lindsey ache even more.

Once Camilla's orgasm passed, Camilla began working her fingers on Lindsey's folds again. Lindsey bucked against her until she was right back at the edge.

"Mistress, please," she said. "May I come for you?"

"Yes," Camilla whispered.

This time when Lindsey came, it was like a slow tidal wave of bliss that stretched out endlessly until Lindsey was sure that she'd passed into some other plane.

She sank back onto the bed with a sigh. Camilla reached across the bed to shut the curtains around them, then lay back down and nestled in close to Lindsey.

Lindsey leaned over and kissed her. "Thank you, Mistress."

"No." Camilla drew her thumb down Lindsey's cheek. "Thank you."

"For what?"

Camilla planted a soft kiss on Lindsey's forehead. "For giving me the gift of your submission."

EPILOGUE

CAMILLA

*C*amilla held up the leather blindfold. "Put this on."

Lindsey's face turned a delightful shade of crimson. "Isn't it a little early for that? And, right here?" She glanced over at June, who was clearing their breakfast from the table.

Camilla placed her hands on her hips. "Are you questioning your Mistress?"

"No." Lindsey took the blindfold from Camilla and slipped it over her eyes.

"Don't get too excited. I want to show you something, that's all. A surprise." Camilla leaned in and whispered into Lindsey's ear. "Your mind always goes to the dirtiest of places."

The blush on Lindsey's face deepened.

Camilla stifled a chuckle. She just couldn't help herself. Not when Lindsey was so easy to tease. She took Lindsey's hand. "Come with me."

Camilla led Lindsey out of the dining room and up the stairs carefully. They turned and headed left.

"Are we going to the east wing?" Lindsey asked.

"You'll see," Camilla replied.

It was no surprise that Lindsey had figured it out. A couple of months after Lindsey had moved back in, permanently this time, Camilla began to have the east wing cleaned out and renovated. She told Lindsey not to go in there under any circumstances because it was unsafe due to all the work being done, which was partially true.

Lindsey had picked up on the fact that something else was going on. But, ever the obedient submissive, she played along anyway. And Camilla had promised her that it would be worth it in the end. Now, after six months, the wing wasn't yet complete. But that was the point.

Camilla led Lindsey into a vast, empty antechamber which several other rooms branched off. Just a few months ago, this room had been run down, with old, faded wallpaper and a decade of dust coating the floorboards. Now, it looked new and fresh, and more in line with the rest of the house. However, the walls were unpainted, the windows were bare, and there wasn't so much as a light fixture.

"We're here." Camilla removed Lindsey's blindfold.

Lindsey looked around. "Is this the east wing?"

"That's right. But this isn't just the east wing. These are our new rooms."

"Our new rooms?" Lindsey's forehead furrowed. "Why do you want us to move out of your rooms?"

"That's the problem. Those rooms have always been *my* rooms, not ours." Camilla took Lindsey's hands. "I don't want you to feel like you're living in my house. I want us to have a space that belongs to both of us."

"Camilla, I don't know what to say." Lindsey gazed

around, wide-eyed. "Are you really okay with leaving your rooms behind? That's a big change."

Change. Once upon a time, that word terrified Camilla. But Lindsey had changed that. "It was a difficult decision. But I want to build something new with you."

"I want that too," Lindsey said. "This is perfect."

"Of course, it isn't finished. I want us to pick out all the details together. The decor, the furnishings, everything." Camilla pulled Lindsey to the center of the room. "We're going to decorate the entire wing together. Then we're going to finally throw that party we've been talking about for months. Not just a dinner party. A big housewarming celebration."

"That sounds wonderful."

"In fact, I've been thinking it's time we opened up the house more. I want to have more guests and throw more parties. I want to make the manor come alive again, like when I was a child. That is, if it's okay with you."

"I would love that," Lindsey said.

"Of course, we're going to need more staff. Some more help for June, perhaps a full-time chef. But I'm getting ahead of myself."

"No, it's great. I'm happy to see you this excited about something."

"I have some news that's going to make you even happier," Camilla said. "Remember that friend of mine you sent your portfolio to?"

"The one who owns a gallery?" Lindsey asked.

"The very same. She finally had a look at your work, and she was very impressed. She's opening another gallery in the city next year, and she wants your artwork to be in the opening exhibition."

Lindsey beamed. "Seriously?"

"Seriously. She'll get in touch with you soon, but I wanted to be the one to tell you."

"That's amazing." Lindsey slung her arms around Camilla's neck and pressed her lips to Camilla's. "I'm glad you pushed me to work on my art. I'm glad you made me put myself out there."

"This was all you, Lindsey," Camilla said. "It was always you. I gave you a little nudge, but you're the one who chose to take control of your life."

"Well, I couldn't have done it without you. Thank you for encouraging me."

"I did it because I believe in you. And I want the world to see how talented you are." Camilla kissed her again. "Now, why don't I give you a tour of our rooms?"

Camilla led Lindsey to the bedroom and opened the door, revealing a huge, light-filled space much brighter than Camilla's old bedroom. She showed Lindsey their sitting room, and the parlor, and the huge bathroom which made Lindsey squeal with excitement.

"Can we get a bath like the one in your rooms?" she asked.

"We can get an even bigger one." Camilla guided Lindsey back to the antechamber and out into a hallway. "Down this hall is my new study. Your new studio is right across from it." She pointed to the end of the hall. "And through that door is the most important room of all."

Lindsey's eyes lit up. "Do you mean the playroom?"

Camilla nodded.

"Can we go inside?"

"Of course." Camilla put her hand on the small of Lindsey's back and led her to the playroom. "I took the liberty of furnishing it already. I know I said we were going to do this together, but this is the one exception."

"I don't mind, Mistress," Lindsey said.

"I'm sure you'll love what I've done with it." Camilla opened the door and turned on the light.

Lindsey looked around the room. "It's the same?"

Camilla nodded. "I had everything moved in here when you were in the city last week."

And she meant everything. The four-poster canopy bed. All the cabinets and drawers filled with surprises. Even the dark wallpaper was identical.

"Do you like it?" Camilla asked.

"I love it," Lindsey said. "It's perfect."

Camilla walked over to the bed. Sitting on top of the table beside it was the large wooden chest with her initials etched into the lid. She placed the blindfold down next to the chest and opened it up.

Camilla pulled out the blue leather collar, letting it dangle from her finger. She fixed her eyes on Lindsey's. "Do you still think it's 'too early for that?'"

"No, Mistress," Lindsey said. "Not at all."

"Then come here."

A smile played on Lindsey's lips. She shut the door and joined her Mistress by the bed.

ABOUT THE AUTHOR

Anna Stone is the bestselling author of Being Hers. Her lesbian romance novels are sweet, passionate, and sizzle with heat. When she isn't writing, Anna can usually be found relaxing on the beach with a book.
Anna currently lives on the sunny east coast of Australia.

Visit www.annastoneauthor.com for information on her books and to sign up for her newsletter.

facebook.com/AnnaStoneRomance
twitter.com/AnnaStoneAuthor

Printed in Poland
by Amazon Fulfillment
Poland Sp. z o.o., Wrocław